Raphael

AND THE

Noble Task

HARPERCOLLINS*PUBLISHERS*

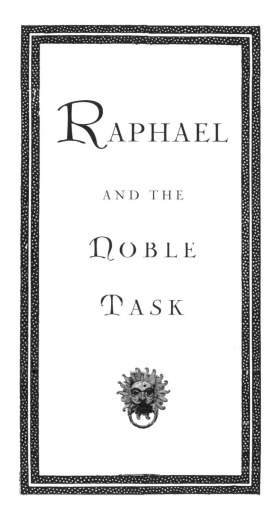

Raphael

AND THE

Noble

Task

CATHERINE A. SALTON

ILLUSTRATIONS BY DAVID WEITZMAN

FIRST EDITION
Library of Congress Cataloging-in-Publication Data
is available upon request

ISBN 0-06-019675-0

00 01 02 03 04 ❖/RRD 10 9 8 7 6 5 4 3 2 1

Book design by Claire Naylon Vaccaro

A Note to the Reader

As this story happens quite a long time ago in an unusual place, a few words may be unfamiliar to the reader.

The word "chimère" is French in origin and is pronounced "shim-AIR." The word "façade" is also French and is said with a soft "c"; thus, "fah-SAHD." The proper name "Madra-Dubh" is Irish Gaelic, and in this case is pronounced "MAHdrah-DOOV." And, finally, the proper name "Æthelred" is Anglo-Saxon, and is simply pronounced "ATHel-red," where the "æ" sounds like the "a" in "apple."

List of Illustrations

All shall be well, and all shall be well,
and all manner of thing shall be well.

JULIAN OF NORWICH

Revelations of Divine Love, ca. 1393

Raphael

AND THE

Noble Task

Chapter One

This is a story about something that happened a very long time ago, at the very top of a Cathedral that stands on the edge of a little town in a country that is very far away.

This particular Cathedral was built over a few hundred years during a period of time which we call the Middle Ages, for lack of anything better to call it. The Middle Ages came after the Golden Age, when people thought about mathematics and ran around naked a lot, and before the Renaissance, when people thought about mathematics again but this time wearing clothes. It is only a small exaggeration to say that during the Middle Ages most people largely forgot about mathematics, except insofar as to use it to build Cathedrals.

Cathedrals are vast and magnificent edifices, meant to reflect the Kingdom of God on earth, and so it took many years to build one. Teams of laborers cut huge blocks of

stone from quarries and dragged them across miles of mud-rutted countryside to the site. Carpenters and roughmasons took the stones and from them formed a cross in the earth, a cross which they raised up into soaring arches, knit together in turn by spreading fans of granite so delicate they look like the fingers of an elm tree in the sky. Inside, the freemasons and hardstone cutters carved rock so unyielding that you can still sharpen knives on it into roses, and leaves, and folds of drapery that look like a breath could move them. And, best of all, these master sculptors carved hundreds of gargoyles, chimères, statues, and tomb effigies, and placed them on every roof and in every corner to be found.

It is with these inhabitants of the Cathedral that our story is concerned.

We begin with the gargoyles. Look along any outside wall of the Cathedral, and you will see them: rows of creatures, monstrous and exotic, peering down at you with open mouths. They are there to protect the Cathedral, but not from you; they are there to protect it from water. That is largely (but not entirely, as you will see) the gargoyles' task.

Placed at strategic points along the gutters of the Cathedral, the gargoyles use their open mouths to direct rainwater away from the vulnerable mortared walls and toward people's heads. That last part may not have been intentional, but for the gargoyles it's the best part of the job. Gargoyles are a little sensitive about looking like they're throwing up all the time and, unfortunately, have become somewhat hostile about it. They're also aware that in the hierarchy of cathedral statuary they carry the anchor, ranking only slightly above graffiti carved in by notables who'd survived some piddling land war in France and felt the need to advertise.

Above gargoyles in Cathedral society are the grotesques, or as they prefer to be called, the chimères. (That's French and it's taken by the gargoyles as yet more evidence of utterly unfounded snobbery.) The chimères are decorative statues that do not serve as waterspouts. Like gargoyles, they're usually monsters of one sort or another, including dragons, griffins, satyrs, and the occasional oddball parandrus. But unlike gargoyles, chimères are not limited by attachment to heavy counterbalancing stones, and so they tend

3

to have more options. This point is lost on people today. We tend to lump both the real gargoyles and the chimères into one group and call them all gargoyles. This might say something about a loss of precision in modern thought but let's not get into that.

Taking the highest rank at the Cathedral are the tomb effigies, which are the stone figures of famous people interred there. Included in this group are the occasional bust or sculpture of an important person, living or dead, and the human faces in the bosses of the vaults, and the people carved into the wooden stalls that line the choir. These figures tend toward the pompous and self-absorbed and generally have little to say to the gargoyles or the chimères.

The religious statues and the stained glass windows are also part of the Cathedral, but they stand outside the rule that I have described, for they are different in nature. All I need to say about them now is that they, like certain other inhabitants of the Cathedral, once helped a chimère who sat on the North Balcony of the North Tower of the West Façade of the Cathedral when this story happened. His name was— and is, still—Raphael.

Chapter Two

It is very important to a chimère to know what he is, so that is where we will begin.

Raphael was basically a griffin. This means that he had a lion's body and legs, with the great arched wings of an eagle flaring from his shoulders. But Raphael was different in one very important respect. Instead of the eagle's head of the ordinary run-of-the-mill griffin, his carver had decided to give him the neck and head of a fierce dragon, and to sculpt delicate scales spreading across his shoulders and down his flanks. The effect was so astonishing that upon seeing it the master stonemason immediately gave Raphael's carver a promotion, a raise, and the day off. Not long after that Raphael was lifted, swaying, high into the air by a precarious wooden hoist and placed in a little niche on the north-side balcony of the West Façade, the magnificent entry into the Cathedral. From his perch Raphael oversaw the largest of the three church doors.

This position—guarding the Great Portal—is a very great honor for a chimère, and Raphael took it seriously. Crouched over a small stone railing, wings spread like he was ready to burst into flight, day in and day out Raphael carefully studied all the people who came to the Cathedral. Although he wasn't certain exactly what he should be guarding against (Raphael was the Cathedral's youngest chimère, as the West Façade of the Cathedral was completed over a hundred years after con struction first began), he felt that if he simply watched long enough, eventually he would understand everything about the place he defended and the people who lived and visited there.

And there were a very many people indeed. Raphael soon determined that they were of two types: the men in the black robes who lived there all the time, and the people who came through the Great Portal and then left again, usually when the great bells in the Spire pealed their call across the town. The men in black robes were called monks, Raphael learned. They ate and slept in the Cloister, a square building tucked into the long south flank of the Cathedral, but spent much of their time inside the great church with the people who visited. They also ran a School, as they were a teaching order. Sometimes the little boys at the School would sneak away from lessons to play in the High Reaches of the Cathedral, and Raphael looked forward to their visits very much, even though he could do nothing but listen and look properly fierce when they were about.

Unlike the monks, the people who visited the Cathedral were of all kinds and came for many reasons. Inspired by the merry talk of the little boys, Raphael would stare in bedazzlement upon the whirl of activity in the Cathedral Square and try to identify them: here a yeoman farmer bringing produce to the monks; there a prosperous wool merchant with his fat-cheeked family; here a bride swept, laughing, up the stairs to the church door; there a doleful thief, newly shriven, on his way to the gallows. Each morning increased Raphael's desire to know more. He thrilled to the cacophony of the market days, when the cobbled Square filled with a confusing splendor of vegetable stalls, lowing cows, bright snapping flags and serenading musicians. He was ferocious when groups of armored men mounted on great stamping horses came pounding at the door of the Cathedral (and was secretly relieved when they departed without incident). He kept vigil during the woeful funeral processions, posed decorously when noblemen made their dignified approach, stood rejoicing during weddings, glared warningly at the catchpurses (known as pickpockets to you and me) who skulked about the Square, and, increasingly, shivered with a longing he didn't understand when the chanting of the monks breathed like gentle smoke through the vaults of the Cathedral.

For the fact was, as the seasons passed, that Raphael had become lonely.

It wasn't as if he were left to his own devices all the time, not at all. There were always the little boys from the School who jumped on his back or played games under his protective vigilance. The monks sometimes came, climbing the staircases on each side of Raphael's balcony, sometimes placing a gentle hand on Raphael's head or paw when they stopped in contemplation. And Raphael found companionship, too, in the little creatures who also lived in the Cathedral: under the generous shelter of his wings, entire clans of church mice and generations of pigeon tribes had been raised. Many nights Raphael would spend in rousing discussions of mouse philosophy or pigeoncraft. But sometimes, even in the midst of the most spirited argument, Raphael would feel the quiet yearning pulling again at his heart. (For, indeed, chimères have hearts, although not of the strictly anatomical kind.) In order to spare his friends his distress, he would turn his face away to the vast night Square.

As you probably have surmised, the time came when Raphael felt that he simply must do something about his condition. It was distracting him from his job. And because he was unusually sensible for someone so young, he decided to start by asking the oldest chimère he knew of in the Cathedral. This was a most unusual chimère, for he wasn't a monster, or a griffin, or anything else like that; he was an old man with a pointed hat who watched over the town from the heights of the Spire. His name was the Alchemist.

Chapter Three

One winter evening, after the sun was safely sent to bed, Raphael left his railing perch and clambered foot over foot, wings over tail, up and down over the soaring roofs of the Cathedral. (For it is a fact, known only to those who frequent Cathedrals, that chimères can freely move about if they wish. It is duty and not necessity that keeps them at their posts.) After much effort and a great deal of scale-raising risk, Raphael finally heaved himself up over the highest railing and plopped down, somewhat flustered, on the topmost narrow balcony of the Spire where the Alchemist held his most grave and thoughtful court.

"Make it short, old chap; I'm a very busy man," said the Alchemist.

Raphael hadn't anticipated this, and so was left speechless for a moment. He thought about asking how the Alchemist could be so busy, considering, but immediately dismissed this as insolent. The night was so cold he could almost hear the stars singing in the sky.

He decided to get to the point. "What is wrong with me?" he asked. "Why do I feel so sad all the time?"

The Alchemist thought for a moment and then nodded briskly. "It's because you have no Task," he harrumphed.

"But I watch the Great Portal—" Raphael began, only to be cut off by the Alchemist's further snort. "Portal indeed," the old man said. "A big hole in the wall, more likely. You be

so kind as to keep an eye on the Philosopher's Stone for a while, that'll keep your mind on your business right certain, I should think."

Raphael had never heard of the Philosopher's Stone, and had no idea anyone was supposed to keep an eye on it. "What's a—"

"The answer to all *their* prayers," sighed the Alchemist dolefully. He sounded as if he were beginning to recite a long-practiced speech, which, in fact, he was. "*They* think that riches are the answer to all questions, as if riches ever actually solved anything, I ask you! Do you see where I am looking? Yes, that corner right there, next to the butcher's, terrible smelly place. Underneath that particular lump of cobblestones—an unattractive lump, I'll admit, almost an aesthetically offensive lump—there is a Stone that will turn lead into gold. It was buried there long ago, when this Cathedral was only a spark in the mind of our great Architect; and, as the Cathedral rose, I—yes, I, a humble Alchemist—was chosen to watch over it, to keep it secret from all."

"Well, you've told *me* about it, haven't you?" asked Raphael, puzzled at how someone could keep something secret by explaining it to anyone who dropped by.

"What need have you for gold?" huffed the Alchemist, for he hadn't thought about that. "You need a Task, as I have; something dreadfully important, something critical to the continued existence of the Celestial Spheres. Like that other chimère, what was his name? Pernifus? Parsinore? Parsifal, that's it. *He* had one."

"Excuse me," said Raphael eagerly, "who was Pars—"

"Never you mind," replied the Alchemist abruptly. "The fact remains that you need a Noble Task. Although you're rather callow for such a thing, I should think. Run along now, you mustn't divide my attention any longer. Good evening."

"Good evening," replied Raphael politely. As he clambered foot over foot, wings over tail, up and down over the slippery steep lead roofs of the Cathedral back to his post on the West Façade, he thought deeply about what the Alchemist had said. He needed a Task, that was certain. But the old chimère hadn't told him how to go about finding one! Who would know where to find a noble Task, an important Task, a Task critical to the continued existence of the Celestial Spheres? And then it struck him. The most noble denizens of the Cathedral would know. He must seek out the tomb effigies.

Chapter Four

nticipation makes a wait five times as long, so Raphael was quite restless and excited by the time the sun finally went down the next evening. As soon as night cloaked the town and the Square emptied of activity, Raphael left his post and crept, foot over slow foot, wings flattened and tail tucked in, across his balcony and down the left-hand spiral staircase step by step until he found himself, for the first time in his life, on the floor of the great Cathedral.

He huddled shivering in the deep shadow of a pier, trying to buck up his courage. The Cathedral made him feel very small indeed. Above him soared the vaults, lost in the darkness over a hundred feet in the air. Far away at the east end of the Cathedral there was a red glow of candleflame; all around him hung the thick, biting smoke of incense. But these things weren't what was frightening. What alarmed

Raphael was that all around him he felt the weight of eyes. The white, blind eyes of cold statues, the bulging eyes of stone demons, the silent pointed faces carved into fanciful flowers, the birds and strange animals cavorting everywhere in the stone, all stared fixedly at him until Raphael was quite overcome with dread. Thinking only of returning to his safe niche on the West Façade, he scrambled in an undignified clattering of claws straight backward, bounced off something that clanged (it was an utterly innocuous metal offering box attached to the wall), lost his footing in a panic, and skidded face first into a small chapel tucked into the South Aisle of the Nave. In it were two tombs, and on them, to Raphael's good fortune, were what he had come for: two life size statues, lying on their backs, in the shape of the people interred inside the stone boxes beneath. In other words, tomb effigies.

"Goodness, who let the cat in here?" complained the nearest effigy. She was a very grand lady. Her hands were primly crossed over her rich draped robe, her delicately shod feet propped up by a silent gilded lion; but there was a tight, pinched expression on her beautiful face that warned of tantrums and hurtful whims.

"It's not a cat, Margaret, it's a gargoyle," humphed the other, a large-jowled knight dressed even more grandly than the lady. "Begone, churl, gargoyles belong not with great ones."

"Please," said Raphael, "I'm not a gargoyle, I'm a chimère, and I've come to ask—"

"Did you hear that? Did you hear that?" shrieked the lady. "The cheek of it, disagreeing with its betters! Do something, Dunstan."

Sir Dunstan, for that was his name, did the only thing he ever did when his wife used that tone of voice: he winced. This simple act put him in a much more generous mood toward Raphael, for he saw that Raphael winced too. And it wasn't often that anyone asked his opinion any more, either. So he said, gruffly but gently, "Hush, Margaret, and let's hear the garg—the shimmy—oh, whatever it is, let's hear it out, shall we?"

Lady Margaret began to quarrel, but Raphael had already leapt at the invitation. "You see, I need to find a Task, sir, a Noble and Critical one, and I thought you would know such things, being noble people and all."

Sir Dunstan looked surprised. "Oh. Well. Noble Task, and all that. Hmm. Well. Have you thought about going on a Quest, perhaps, or a Crusade? Good things, Crusades; come up with a great pile of loot at the end, don't you know."

Raphael's heart sank. "I don't think I could go on a Crusade," he said slowly. "I must defend the Great Portal."

"Ah. Defend. Great Portal. Defending's not bad, really, but you don't get out much, a pity that. Not much loot involved . . . is there?"

Sir Dunstan sounded so hopeful that Raphael felt bad about disappointing him. "None at all, really. But"—and here Raphael looked imploringly at Sir Dunstan—"is loot all that matters in a Noble Task? For if it is, I haven't a hope of finding one."

This seemed to flummox Sir Dunstan. He spluttered for a bit, said "Humph" a few too many times, muttered "Task. Task," under his breath, and finally ground to a befuddled halt. This gave Lady Margaret her much-desired opening and she seized it with a will.

"Noble Task! I haven't ever heard such foolishness!" she cried. "Piffling about on horses, guzzling ale in taverns, leaving me alone to take care of everything—Noble Task, my noble foot, what *I* do is the Noble Task! You try giving birth and caring for a passel of mewling brats and a great drafty barn of a house (that was no manor, Dunstan, that was a castle-sized cowshed, that's what it was) while the servants—well, you just can't get good help anymore! And these sniveling monks with their long noses stuck in books daring to lecture me, me, Lady Dunstan, about Noble Tasks—I've never been so insulted in my life, except for now!"

Lady Margaret clacked on, but Raphael's ears had perked up at the mention of books and Noble Tasks. His hopes soared. If monks heard about them from books, and there were monks here in the Cathedral, then there might be books as well! In a fire of excitement he turned to go, but caught himself when he realized he hadn't yet made a proper farewell. He tried to catch Sir Dunstan's attention in order to say a polite "Good evening."

But Raphael soon found that Sir Dunstan had quite forgotten all about him. The noble knight and his lady wife were much too busy for good-byes, as they were squabbling peevishly over things that had passed away many years before. Raphael eventually gave up trying to make himself heard and left them to their endless quarrel. He had only one thing on his mind as he ascended the spiral staircase: the next night he simply had to find the Cathedral's books.

Chapter Five

Now to us, finding books in a Cathedral is a simple thing. One just pops over to the Visitors' Center, pays a fee for a map, and takes a nice amble to the Library (or the Scriptorium, as the case may be). But, at the time of this story, there was no Visitors' Center and certainly no map, fee or no fee, so Raphael was left entirely to his own devices.

Usually, if he were curious about something in the Cathedral, he would ask the mice. Cathedral mice know everything, because, quite honestly, they are everywhere; every part of the church has its own mouse society. In the crypt below, the walls and the chapels above that, in the stone tracery of the columns and the windows, and in the kitchens, and storehouses, and gardens of the Cloister, the mice live and work and study. Raphael was most familiar with the High Reaches mouse clan. But as all mice consider themselves part of a greater family, any Cathedral mouse would have been happy to help him.

The problem was that it was the dead of winter, and all the local mouse societies had moved from the bitter cold of the towers and buttresses to their winter homes snug inside the Cloister. Raphael looked and looked but there was not a mouse to be found on the West Façade. The pigeons, though they tried to help, knew only those inside parts of the Cathedral that they could see through the windows, and so had nothing to offer him. And to go back inside to try to find the books himself—alone in the darkness, with all those blank eyes studying his every move—why, that was simply impossible.

There was only one alternative left. He must speak to the gargoyles.

So very late the next night, well after the moon had set and darkness lay like a cloak over the quiet town, Raphael padded softly to the promontory on the far corner of his balcony and sat down very neatly and politely. He cleared his throat to let the gargoyle know he was there.

"Good evening," said Raphael to the gargoyle.

"Get lost, you great silly git," replied the gargoyle smartly. Now this is a perfectly dreadful thing to say to anyone, but it's a standard opening gambit in gargoyle conversation, so Raphael wasn't put off in the least.

"How goes it on the buttresses?" he inquired, figuring that asking someone about his job is generally an inoffensive way to begin asking for a favor. And in most ordinary circumstances he would have been right, but gargoyles are certainly not ordinary, as they will assure you themselves.

"Not blasted well, considering some great snakey statue is prancing about like a fairy princess, you enormous batwinged numbwit," came the immediate retort. A chorus of raucous laughter from the other gargoyles followed this riposte. The first gargoyle, whose name was Madra-Dubh (an overly complicated way of saying "black dog"), beamed at his compatriots on the ramparts and waited eagerly for Raphael to say something else.

Raphael steeled his resolve. "You see, I'm trying to find something, and I think you might know where it is," he said as quickly as possible.

"Oooh, and it's trying to find something," crowed Madra-Dubh as the others cackled gleefully. "Not good enough for the fawning idle-headed dewberry to sit on its donkey-spotted behind and do its right job, mark me! Nooo, it's got to go thumping about pestering the working folk with foolish don't-you-knows. Go drop some feathers, ye molting chicken-witted dragglebeak, and leave us in peace then." He took a grand bow as approving cries of "Deadly!" and "Hear, hear!" rose from the railings and buttresses of the other gargoyles. But as he opened his long pointed dog face to follow up with a *truly* devastating insult, he was seized with a terrible fit of coughing that nearly shook him off his corbel.

Raphael, now discouraged, had just decided to go back to his niche when this happened. He saw that Madra-Dubh seemed to be choking on something caught in his open throat. This is an occupational hazard for gargoyles, as whatever comes sliding down the roofs and gutters of the Cathedral eventually slides off through a gargoyle's gaping mouth, and sometimes things can get stuck. Raphael became alarmed as the gargoyle gasped and wheezed.

"Can I help you?" he asked. Madra-Dubh shook his head violently, as he was unable to speak for gagging. When he could gasp a breath, the gargoyle croaked, in as dignified a fashion as he could, "None of your concern, newtnose—bit of lead broke off the roof ridge, got wedged—"

Raphael saw that the gargoyle's legs weren't long enough to let him get the metal out himself. And as gargoyles, unlike chimères, are attached to a heavy counterbalancing block of stone which prevents them from moving around freely (a particularly sore point between the two tribes), none of Madra-Dubh's fellows could help either. It was a terrible quandary. The gargoyle was obviously in great distress, and yet to try to help him might make him even more furious. But Madra-Dubh kept coughing and choking; it seemed to be getting worse.

Well, Raphael thought after a minute of dancing from foot to foot with indecision, *if he won't help me, he won't help me no matter what I do.* So he leaped nimbly atop the corbel, flaring his wings out for balance, and teetered foot over foot out to where Madra-Dubh clung. In an instant he had hooked the stubborn bit of metal with his claw and started pulling on it with all his might.

"Are ye blooming *daft?*" shrieked the gargoyle and instantly tried to throw him off. Raphael hooked his other paw over the gargoyle's head and held on for dear life. Madra-Dubh's mad thrashing and coughing spasm had one useful side effect, though, for the metal was quickly dislodged and came out of the gargoyle's throat with an audible pop. Raphael snatched it up and scrambled backward onto the balcony, his heart pounding, his tail puffed out and every scale standing on end.

All around was a clamoring of insult as every gargoyle on the West Façade lit into him as loudly as possible for his "toffee-brained impertinence" and his "billowing toadfoot arrogance" and advised him in the strongest possible terms, not repeatable in this polite company, to drop dead already. But Madra-Dubh, after he'd finished coughing, was silent. He'd seen the sharp-edged piece of metal in Raphael's claws and had realized that if it had stayed in his throat, it might very well have caused a tiny crack. Tiny cracks let water in, and freezing water is one of the two things that gargoyles fear most of all, for, as it remorselessly expands, it can eventually break apart a whole gargoyle.

So Madra-Dubh, despite knowing that he'd get nothing but grief from the other gargoyles, decided to do something no gargoyle had done in a hundred years. He swiveled his head back and forth, fixing his howling compatriots with a steely glare, and barked, "Shush your gaping yaps, ye worthless gits, I'm speaking to the gentleman here." The cacophony was instantly quelled. "Well, what's the piffling harpy need to find, then?" he said to Raphael, with somewhat exaggerated patience.

"Books," said Raphael delightedly. "Do you know where books are in the Cathedral?"

Madra-Dubh furrowed his dog face gravely. "Not off the top of the head," he admitted. "We'll have to use the All's-Well, I should think." And immediately he bent himself forward just as far as he could go, opened his toothy jaws wider than he'd ever done, and bellowed into the darkness, "ALL'S

WELL ON THE WEST FAÇADE AND WHERE'S THE BLASTED BOOKS IN THIS BLOOMING FROZEN BARN, ME NAVE LADS?"

And from around the corner, only slightly fainter, immediately came the raspy reply, "ALWAYS WANTING SOMETHING, AREN'T WE? ALL'S WELL ON THE NORTH NAVE AND WHERE'S THE BLASTED BOOKS IN THIS BLOOMING FROZEN BARN, NORTH TRANSEPT?"

Raphael listened in amazement as the message was relayed from gargoyle to gargoyle, becoming progressively more muffled with distance until it dwindled away into the hush of the night. There followed quite a long wait in absolute silence. As Madra-Dubh simply sat perfectly still on his corbel, Raphael decided he'd sit patiently too, even as the minutes stretched into hours and Raphael began to worry about getting back to his niche before dawn.

Finally, only minutes before the sun began cresting over the town, Raphael heard it: a nearly inaudible call from far away across the roofs, that was repeated somewhat louder somewhat closer, and then louder yet and closer yet. He bolted to his feet, shivering with eagerness, as finally the call was shouted in magnificent frog-throated chorus from only a few buttresses away: "ALL'S WELL FROM THE CLOISTER-MEN, AND THE BLASTED BOOKS IN THIS BLOOMING FROZEN BARN ARE WELL AND GOOD IN THE

SOUTH CLOISTER CHAMBER, NOT THAT IT'S ANY OF YOUR BUSINESS, YOU IGNORANT MUD-WATTLED NITS."

"I suppose you got that," remarked Madra-Dubh.

"Oh yes! Thank you so much! Thank you all!" cried Raphael. And even though the winter dawn was cold as a knife blade when it touched his niche, Raphael felt nothing but a fierce glow of warmth and joy. Surely now he would find his Noble Task!

Chapter Six

Now in case you've never heard of the Gargoyle All's-Well, here is what happened. When, in a nonemergency situation, certain information needs to be passed among the gargoyles, they will shout to each other from buttress to buttress all the way around the entire Cathedral until the answer is found.

So when Madra-Dubh started the All's-Well with Raphael's inquiry about the books, it bounced all the way from the West Façade, up the north side of the long Nave wall, around the crosspiece that is the North Transept, up the Choir, around the arc of the Lady Chapel at the far east end, down the other side of the Choir, and around the south side of the Transept again, until it finally reached the gargoyles in the Cloister. (It did spend some time rattling around the Spire gargoyles, which accounts for some of the delay.) The Cloister gargoyles had a vague idea that there were books about, as they had seen some of the monks holding them on occasion, but had no idea where they were specifically kept. Accordingly, it took some time before one of them managed to get the attention of a Dormitory watchmouse scuttling across the icy garden on his way home to his family. The watchmouse in turn conferred with some of the elder mice in the Dormitory mouse society, who were somewhat irritated about being woken up for such an ordinary question, but returned the answer in good time to the Cloister gargoyle, who in turn passed it on.

But I must tell you how Raphael took this news. As you might expect, he spent the entire day in a frenzy of anticipation, barely able to keep himself from dashing headlong across the rooftops of the Cathedral to the Cloister and searching until he found the books he so desperately wanted. Only his profound sense of duty to the Cathedral's defense—and the sure knowledge that he would frighten the wits out of anyone who saw him cavorting on the rooftops— kept him steady at his post. He also kept catching Madra-Dubh looking at him with sly amusement, so there may have been a bit of injured pride involved as well.

It seemed to take forever before the shadows crept up the glowing sunset stone of the West Façade and the town sank into night. At last Raphael was free to seek his heart's desire. To the sound of Madra-Dubh's cackling laughter, the young chimère folded up his wings tight against his back and sprinted across the High Reaches (nodding politely to each amazed gargoyle and chimère he passed, for despite his urgency he was a very-well-brought-up chimère) until he found himself, breathless and dizzy with excitement, clinging to a stone lintel only inches above the massive wooden door into the South Cloister.

"God's nightshirt!" came a tiny outraged exclamation behind him. "State your business, stranger!"

Startled, Raphael had to scrabble wildly to keep from falling off the lintel. He turned to see a watchmouse (as it happened, it was the very same Dormitory watchmouse from the All's-Well the night before) confronting him. The watchmouse's whiskers bristled with alarm and his tail was stiff as a swizzle stick. This is not nearly as funny as it sounds, for watchmice are the most fearless fighters in the Cathedral when matters warrant.

"I'm Raphael, a chimère from the West Façade," Raphael hurriedly explained, drawing himself up into a posture he hoped looked mature and responsible. "I'm trying to find the books in the South Cloister. Are they here?"

The unguarded hope in Raphael's face was so convincing that the watchmouse relaxed. "So it's you that's causing all the fuss," he said. "You'll be wanting the Scriptorium. Through that door and down the hall, first door on your right, and"—he shuddered visibly—"*don't be waking up the dog,* do you hear?"

Raphael nodded and without further ado leapt silently down to the ground. As he pushed through the door, the watchmouse muttered, "Great beaky face and all those claws, like to give a watchmouse a heart condition," but Raphael, in his excitement, heard nothing but the creaking of the hinges and then the sound of his claws rustling softly in the dry rushes strewn on the floor of the Cloister corridor.

He paused for a long moment before the first door on the right. Behind it was the fulfillment of his great desire; the thing that would fill to overflowing the aching emptiness in his heart. The heavy iron-clad portal was slightly ajar. Raphael pushed his nose into the opening and slipped through.

Directly before him, with his back to the chimère, was a man sitting at a desk.

Raphael froze in terror. How could any of the monks be up at this hour?! In a panic, he scuttled into the deep shadow of the nearest corner and huddled in a miserable ball. The next few minutes were agonizing as he waited for his inevitable discovery. But as time passed and the man sat unmoving, Raphael's terror slowly drifted away. He began to study the black-robed figure with curiosity and, finally, sympathy.

For the man seemed to be in great distress. He cupped his head in his hands as he studied a large open book, filled with neat lines and figures drawn carefully in black ink. A single candle guttered before him. The flame flickered briefly as the man sighed.

"Dear Saint Lawrence," said the man into the silence, the shadows of the candle dancing wildly about him, "if there was ever a time to help your children, this is it." He stood up abruptly, his hands falling to his sides—Raphael felt a brief resurgence of panic—but then sat down again and dropped his heavy head back into his palms. "This cold will never end, and there will soon be no food for anyone. How will I feed my abbey and the poor as well? If one more child is abandoned here, I will have nothing to give it."

The man had a right to be troubled, for he was Abbot Gregory, the director of the Cathedral Abbey and the head of the Cathedral School, and many people depended upon him for their very lives. Abbot Gregory was responsible for the administration of every task and the well-being of every person who lived and worked at the Cathedral. Like Raphael, he took his obligations very seriously, but things were working against him this winter. The harvest had been very poor, due to late rains that rotted the crops in the fields, and Abbot Gregory could see from the account books in front of him that all too soon the Abbey's stores would be exhausted. This was a very grim prospect indeed. Monks and little growing boys cannot live on prayers alone, and soon that would be all that Gregory had to give them.

"Help me," said the Abbot to the shadows. He closed the

book and tucked it under one arm. Raphael thought that he looked terribly old as he watched the Abbot rise from his chair. In fact he was a young man to us—only thirty-five— but his face was deeply lined in the candlelight, and his short-cropped hair was salted with gray.

Perhaps it was the blackness of the corner in which Raphael hid, or perhaps it was the weight of his worries. Whatever it was, the Abbot looked right past Raphael without seeing him as he turned and tread heavily into the darkness beyond his desk. At the last moment he turned back and pinched out the candle.

Raphael, still huddled very small, saw a dim slash of light open into the other end of the room. It first illuminated a fireplace in the stone wall, which he saw was still glowing faintly with banked coals, and then—and then!—it raked over several desks. Upon each of the desks was a book. With a hard creaking sound, the long rectangle of light folded in on itself and disappeared with a bang. Abbot Gregory, still desperately seeking hope in the midst of the darkness, had at last gone to bed.

Chapter Seven

R aphael was alone with the books.

In most ordinary circumstances, perhaps Raphael would have spent more time considering the plight of Abbot Gregory, and through him the Abbey itself. Certainly later his response would have been different. But he was a very young chimère at the time of this story. He believed (as some people still do even though they are much older and ought to know better) that the things he wanted were the most important things in the world. So as soon as he thought it was safe, he scrambled headlong for the first of the desks that he had seen when Abbot Gregory had left the room.

Chimères can see perfectly well in the dark once their eyes adjust, as you'll agree once you think about what they have to do; so he found the book without stumbling about, and opened it. What he saw was beautiful. It was a single letter "I," drawn in many blazing colors, wrapped with graceful interlocking vines, in which cavorted glowing gold horses and flame-winged birds. Next to it in rigorous ranks were other letters, all looking like sharp thrusts and stabs on the fragile paper, which marched down the page until they met a flowing border of bright green leaves that swept around the edges like the most gracious weeping willow you have ever seen.

Raphael gazed at the book and waited politely.

When nothing happened, he turned the page, thinking that he had not approached the book properly. He waited again, but the tome remained silent. The chimère even cleared his throat gently, *ahem,* thinking to gain its attention that way; but the only sound he heard in response was the gentle tapping of his claw on the parchment.

Puzzled, he began carefully turning the pages. Each looked the same: a lovely drawing, shimmering with color and detail, the ranks of letters, the border. Sometimes in the margin were tiny cramped notations in red ink. And then the blank end page, followed by the heavy leather of the back cover. He reopened the book to that first, radiant "I" and gazed at it with increasing consternation. What was the matter? Why did the book not speak to him?

For you see, Raphael could not read; and Raphael had not realized that books do not speak to you unless you can. With a terrible foreboding he rushed to the book on the next desk.

The same result obtained. He went through every book on every desk in the Scriptorium. Drawings. Letters. Borders. Not a word issued forth from these glorious manuscripts. By the time he reached the final book on the final desk, he understood at last that the books would not reveal their secrets to him, and he was plunged into despair. His dream of a Noble Task was ebbing away, leaving only the void. It was in this state of ravaged hopelessness that he opened the last book and saw the picture that would change everything.

It was a man in brilliant silver armor. His eyes were rolled upward toward the sky, and around his head the air glowed gold. With one massive fist he thrust a sword downward into the writhing coils of a dragon. The dragon snarled and slashed, trying to reach and destroy some children cowering behind the man; but it was clear that the man was on the side of Good, and no dragon could possibly overcome him.

Raphael had seen himself reflected more than once in the windows of the Cathedral. As he stared transfixed at the picture, a thought came to him, as if from very far away: *That dragon looks like me.*

And if this were not enough, other horrible thoughts then came crowding thick and fast. If that dragon looked like Raphael, and that dragon was evil, then . . . could the Alchemist have been wrong? Perhaps Raphael could not have a Noble Task at all—perhaps he was supposed to be the enemy

in someone else's Noble Task—perhaps this picture meant that he was evil, too.

"But I'm *not* evil," Raphael blurted out into the empty Scriptorium. And even though he tried very hard not to, he started to cry.

If something terrible like this has ever happened to you, you know that the first thing you want to do is run away; and run away is what Raphael did. Ashamed of his weeping, but unable to stop, the young chimère bolted from the Scriptorium. He did not care that his claws echoed on the stone, or that the Scriptorium door banged loudly behind him. The only thing he could think about was hiding from the shame and humiliation that were swallowing him up. He tore the door to the Cloister open and dashed outside, not caring where he was going.

The Dormitory watchmouse, warned by the noise of Raphael's frantic flight, knew at once that something had gone seriously awry inside the Scriptorium. He had just scuttled down to the ground from his post on the lintel when the Cloister door opened abruptly and Raphael burst out. Now the watchmouse had his own children, and he recognized an upset young person when he saw one; so he was concerned, not angry, when the Raphael narrowly missed squashing him. "Eh, now, what's the matter?" he called, but Raphael could not speak. He just shook his head, an expression of perfect misery on his face, and turned to run on.

By the time he realized that he had no idea where he was running to, Raphael was lost.

He slowed to a stumbling walk, and then stopped completely. All around him were the yawning caverns of the Cathedral. He must have dashed through the North Cloister and from there into the Cathedral itself, but his path was only a fearful blur to him now. He was in a part of the great church that he did not recognize, and he had no idea of which way would lead back to his safe niche on the West Façade. He wanted so much to go home. Helpless, he took a few steps this way, and then that, but he only ended up more confused and frightened than he had been before.

In the darkness pressing down upon him he felt again the cold contempt of the eyes. Raphael called desperately to them, "Please help me—please, I want to go home," but the faces carved into the stone replied only with mocking sneers. Raphael searched the carvings and colonnades frantically for someone, anyone, who might be kind. At last he spotted a little stone lizard, crouched in a forest of leaves atop a niche much like Raphael's. "Please help me, brother," he said, and his heart leapt with hope when the little lizard turned its cold marble face to him.

"Best flee, you ugly creature," it hissed, "it's time for Vigils, and they'll burn you when they find you."

"Oh no," Raphael whimpered, for he heard something behind him just as the cruel little lizard spoke. It was the heavy shuffling of feet treading on stairs. For Vigils is the night service of the monks, and they were coming into the Cathedral to sing. If they should see Raphael, all would be lost.

Raphael bolted. The columns flashed by him in the heaving blur of nightmares. He ran until he found a dark little hole and into it he burrowed, curling himself up as small as he could, his eyes squeezed shut. There he waited for the end.

But what happened next was not the end at all.

For what Raphael heard was not the hue and cry of his discovery. It was instead a soft thread of voices joined together, singing a music of praise so old that the ancient stone of the Cathedral seemed to awaken to it. The voices grew stronger and spread in slow waves out from the choir. They rose and fell in the darkness, as insistent as the tides of a warm sea, until the echoing spaces of the Cathedral itself took up the voices and sang with them. The music stole over Raphael and washed away his terror, bit by bit, replacing it with a stillness, the kind that comes after you have been hurt or frightened and cried for a very long time.

Raphael listened quietly. He did not notice the iciness of the stone floor beneath him or the thick darkness all around him. He simply lay silently until after a while he felt not nearly so afraid, and thought that he might open his eyes. He found that he'd tucked himself under a heavy wooden chair in the center of a small stone room. On a tiny ledge in the wall before him a small candle burned without flickering. Above it were three tall stained glass windows, each containing the image of a great, white-robed angel. The one on the left held an open book; the one on the right carried a huge trumpet across its chest; and the one in the center held a sprig of herbs in one hand while the other was raised in a benediction. As they gazed down at Raphael, their regard was not stern or terrible, but instead calm and kind. And in the middle of those three windows, warmed in the steady pool of candlelight, stood a small statue.

Something about the statue called to the young chimère. Raphael crept out from his hiding place and took a hesitant step toward the figure. As he did, a scent of incense and beeswax surrounded him like a cloud. The world itself seemed to fade away in the fragrance and the deep insistence of the monks' chant. He took another step closer to the statue.

A young woman with a gentle expression gazed out at him from the darkness. Her plain blue gown fell in folds to her bare feet, and her hair was unbound, spreading over her shoulders in a rippling veil. In her arms she cradled a baby, who reached up with one small hand to touch her face in a gesture of calm devotion. As Raphael stood wondering, his head cocked to one side, he felt as if his hurt and disappointment were being softly lifted away. For the young woman seemed to speak to him in a manner he did not fully understand; she did not move, nor did she actually say a word, but all the same, she told Raphael a long and beautiful story. In the icy darkness of that chapel, she spoke gently to Raphael alone. She spoke of joy in good times, and patience in hard, and of hope even in the bleakest hours of all.

It was much later before Raphael realized that he must return to his post on the West Façade. He was very cold as he turned away. But even though he could not exactly remember the story the lady told him, he felt greatly heartened, and he knew without thinking the right way to go to get home. He left the Lady Chapel without fear and walked quietly through the shadows to the Transept staircase, which would take him to the High Reaches. And for once, as he walked, he did not feel the weight of the eyes.

There was one set of eyes that did take surprised notice of Raphael, however. A very bleary Abbot Gregory, preparing to return to his quarters, caught just a glimpse of

Raphael before the darkness swallowed him up. The Abbot stared puzzled for a moment until he shook his head to try to clear the cobwebs. *Goodness, that was a big rat,* he thought as he treaded the night stairs leading back to the Dormitory. *What are THEY eating that WE don't know about?*

Chapter Eight

The winter deepened.

Ice crawled relentlessly down the roof-lines, smothering the metal and stone with a frozen rime that the weak sun did nothing to remit. The High Reaches were a frigid wasteland. The pigeons had long since fled downward to the houses, seeking the faint heat from the hearthfires inside. Behind the Cloister walls the mice shivered along with the monks. The Cathedral Square held no music but the howling wind, a wind which sang of nothing but hunger, and cold, and endless darkness.

It was a terrible time for everyone in the Cathedral, but most terrible for Raphael. He had no companions to keep up his spirits. Although he tried once or twice to call to Madra-Dubh, the gargoyle had retreated into a sullen muteness and would not respond to the chimère's greetings. So Raphael was left alone, day after bitter day, to brace himself against the unrelenting wind as he guarded the Cathedral. And in that time he could not help but think of his resemblance to the evil dragon in the monks' book. It was much like prodding a sore tooth, or picking at a scab, but worse in the end; for this was a wound to Raphael's heart, and those can do much more damage when they are not allowed to heal.

Raphael sensed that his obsession was not good for him and for many days he tried to fight it. Every time he felt that he was evil, or could not have a Noble Task, or felt perilously on the edge of despair, he called to mind the young mother in the Lady Chapel. When he did, his fear would fall away and he would feel refreshed in his resolve. But as each new dawn brought nothing but unbroken silence and merciless cold, it was ever so slightly harder to muster the determination to remember what he could of the lady's lovely tale. Gradually, it became too much of an effort to think of good things; yet as always, the sad and bitter thoughts remained easy to bring to mind. Thus it was not long before the desolation outside had crept inside the young chimère as well.

It was in this state that Raphael's good heart, so weakened by his loss of hope, nearly failed him.

The evening was raw. For once the wind had stilled, but the sun was smothered in black clouds threatening sleet. A heavy fog rose from the slick stones of the Cathedral Square, so thick that Raphael could not see across to the shopfronts on the other side. It seemed that time itself had stopped in a falling darkness, neither day nor night. Raphael looked down on this unearthly scene of silent, shifting mists and held his breath, for he heard the clop and jingle of a horseman coming.

Slowly, deliberately, the horseman approached. The sound of the horse's hooves became sharp as the beast left the High Street and entered the Square. Raphael strained his eyes but could see nothing but fog curling sluggishly in the gloom. And then he saw one spot that was a little darker than the rest. It loomed larger with each hard report of the horse's steps, coalescing out of the boiling tendrils of mist. It was a hulking shadow of a knight on a horse. It stopped in the very center of the Square and looked up at the West Façade.

Raphael stared wide-eyed as the fog parted before him to reveal that the knight wore silver armor and the warhorse was brilliant white.

It was as if the picture from the book had sprung to horrible life. An overwhelming desire to run and hide screamed inside him. His claws sprang out and his wings started to clutch to his sides, but he pushed them out again, trembling with terror, clutching the railing with all his might to keep from bolting away. It was a ghastly struggle that Raphael fought alone on the High Reaches. All the shame and loneliness and fear of the last weeks roared up at him at once and very nearly carried him away. So when the knight reached to his side and pulled out his sword as he urged his horse forward, Raphael could not help but close his eyes to wait for the end of what was certainly the knight's Noble Task.

With his eyes squeezed tightly shut, he did not see the knight dismount from his horse. Nor did he see the knight shove the sword into a scabbard on the far side of the saddle, turn, and walk heavily up the stairs into the Cathedral. When he opened his eyes again, Raphael saw only a warhorse standing at the foot of the West Façade with one hind leg cocked idly and no knight anywhere in evidence. From this he drew the conclusion that the Silver Knight was coming up to the High Reaches to kill him, and at that point he lost all hope.

Raphael could not have been more wrong. The knight in question was Earl Odo, the great-great-great-grandson of Sir Dunstan (whose tomb effigy we have previously met), and he had no interest in Raphael at all. In fact, he had come to visit Abbot Gregory on a matter of no small import. Earl Odo had just done something he had sworn a mighty oath that he would never, ever do again, and in an attempt to assure forgiveness he had decided to give a large sum of money to the Abbey.

As Raphael trembled far overhead, Abbot Gregory and Earl Odo sat down to work things out. Earl Odo shamefacedly admitted what he'd been up to, and asked Gregory if a certain sum in gold coin would clear the slate, as it were. Abbot Gregory sighed and explained to Earl Odo that you can't buy God off with cash, but Odo would hear none of that; he traveled in circles where a well-timed gift to one's superior could make the difference between continued favor and getting squashed like a bug, and he wasn't about to change his strategy now. Unable to make a dent in Odo's stubbornness, Gregory at last gave up. He determined that the Earl was truly sorry for what he did and sent him on his way forgiven. Behind him the Earl left his guilt and an impressively large pile of gold.

Abbot Gregory himself was of two minds about this gift. It wasn't right to take money for forgiveness, however fine a point you put on it; but this money would let him send away for food to save his Abbey, and this thought made his heart as light as Earl Odo's purse. *I'll have to confess this,* thought Gregory ruefully, wandering up to the Great Portal to watch Earl Odo heave himself up onto his horse. *But truly, it looks like I've been saved.*

Far above his head on the West Façade, a young chimère watched with amazed relief as the Silver Knight wheeled his alabaster stallion and vanished at a gallop back into the fog. Raphael was thinking the same thing.

Chapter Nine

Raphael's relief lasted only a moment before it was replaced by a wave of shame. He had ducked and tried to hide, hadn't he? He had almost bolted from his post! He had closed his eyes and refused to face the danger! How could someone like him possibly be fit to guard the Cathedral? And then, inevitably, he thought about the evil dragon in the book. Perhaps his cowardice proved that he was like that dragon after all. The Silver Knight hadn't been able to find him this time, but he would certainly come back, and then Raphael would get what he deserved.

We, of course, understand that Raphael was being much too hard on himself. He should have realized that in staying where he was, despite his very real (although mistaken) terror, he had done something so brave and true that he certainly wasn't evil and he certainly was suited for his post. But this simple forgiving thought could not penetrate his self-reproach. Raphael was trapped in his misery, simply because he'd taken a single pebble of doubt from the picture in the book and painstakingly built from it a mighty fortress of despair. The next few days were much longer than I can possibly describe.

It was in this state that Raphael, watching dully over the West Façade on yet another brutal night, saw a woman bring a bundle to the great door of the Cathedral.

The woman's face was hidden by a tattered cloak as she slowly mounted the steps, clutching what looked to be a little heap of cloth to her bosom. A tiny spark of interest was kindled in Raphael as she sank down on the top step and rocked back and forth, her head bowed. Next to her was a small wooden box set within the stone. This was the foundling box, placed there by the monks for babies whose parents could not feed them or take care of them. There was a slender cord above the box which, when pulled, would ring a small bell in the Cloister. Many babies had come into the monks' care this way over the years; but as the woman simply sat next to the box, swaying gently, Raphael could not figure out what she was doing.

His blank dejection at last burned away by curiosity, Raphael folded his wings and crept quietly down from his niche to the topmost point of the Great Portal. From there he could see the woman very well. She was extremely young, almost a child herself, but she was dressed in the heavy black clothing of a widow. Her face was streaked with tears and she spoke out loud to no one, or so Raphael thought.

"I must leave you here," she wept. "I cannot let you starve too. The monks will care for you until I can come back for you. I will come back, I promise. I will find work somehow and then I will come back for you." She placed the bundle carefully into the foundling box, trying to smile, and then snatched it up again and cradled it in her arms. The cloth covering the bundle fell away and Raphael saw what it was she held.

It's a baby! Raphael gasped with shock. *She is leaving her baby here!*

Raphael's mind began to spin. He knew about such things, as some of the little boys who had played about him in the High Reaches were the happy products of just such a surrendering. But as he studied the woman hugging the child, who smiled and burbled joyfully at her, suddenly Raphael found himself back in the Scriptorium. He heard again Abbot Gregory speaking to the shadows: *"This cold will never end, and there will soon be no food for anyone. How will I feed my abbey and the poor as well? If one more child is abandoned here, I will have nothing to give it."*

Raphael gazed at the baby with dawning horror. *There will be nothing to give it,* he thought. *The baby will starve!* Raphael did not know about Earl Odo's gift, nor that Father Gregory had used it days ago to buy food from another town not suffering from famine; he had no idea that even now, mere days away, a young merchant named Nicholas of Bedford urged his sleepy guards and oxdrivers through the night to reach the Cathedral with packs and wagons full of food. Raphael believed only that the baby would die if left in the monks' care. The thought panicked him.

What to do? What to do? And then a thought struck him. It struck him with the force of the sound of the biggest bell in the Cathedral on the biggest feast day of the year, the kind of crashing roar that wallops you like a physical blow, and it went like this: *Maybe this is my Noble Task!*

Why couldn't it be? After all, the monks couldn't take care of the baby. Someone had to, and Raphael was right there! But still, to do such a thing was unheard of! Raphael hesitated, torn by doubt. And then another thought came to him, a thought which may not have been quite as virtuous as the others, but which overwhelmed him all the same. *When the Silver Knight returns,* Raphael told himself, *he will see me tending the baby when no one else could, and he will surely know then that I am not evil!* This must be it! This must be Raphael's Noble Task!

Raphael's heart sang with joy while the woman below him cried. He waited, trembling with anticipation, until she put the baby down again in the foundling box. He danced with impatience as she stood, pulled her hood up over her red hair, squared her shoulders with desperate determination, and pulled the bell cord. Deep inside the Cloister, a small bronze bell clanked insistently and then fell silent.

The woman fled down the steps. Raphael poised himself to jump. And this is what you would have seen, had you been there watching in the great Square of the Cathedral that fateful night: the young woman, whose name was Juliana, flying across the cobblestones as if the Furies themselves were pursuing her; a slender flare-winged shadow springing from the top of the Great Portal and landing atop the steps, peering into the box, and seizing up a small bundle to itself; the Great Portal creaking slowly open just as the shadow bounds impossibly up the sheer face of stone to disappear into darkness; an old monk peering squint-eyed out the door and stepping outside, but finding nothing; the massive door slowly closing; Juliana turning at last at the edge of the Square, her hands clutched to her mouth, seeing a black robe sweeping inside the Cathedral, the door booming shut, and an empty box on the step outside.

Chapter Ten

It is all very well to find one's Noble Task, but then there is the matter of actually performing it. Raphael came face-to-face with this problem when, at last safe in his niche, he gently pulled away the cloth and looked closely at the baby.

Two enormous saucer eyes goggled back at him. They grew even wider as they traveled up Raphael's long pointed nose, to the slanted eyes, from there to the triangular ears, down the scaly snakelike neck, and finally around to the scimitar claws that carefully held the blanket away. The baby's eyebrows shot up to an unlikely height. Raphael took this as an invitation to introduce himself and smiled ingratiatingly.

The baby took one look at Raphael's yawning toothy grin and emitted a shattering howl.

Shocked beyond belief at the extraordinary noise, Raphael sat back so hard he nearly dropped the baby. The screams ricocheted off the stone, bouncing around the High Reaches loudly enough, it seemed, to raise the dead. At any rate, they startled several dozing gargoyles wide awake and caused at least one watchmouse (a different one this time) to jump practically out of his skin. As the shrieks continued unabated, a low rumble of "What's that?" and "Good grief!" and other flustered exclamations began to rise from every corbel, balcony, and buttress on the West Façade.

Raphael was wild to stop the noise. He had no idea of what he'd done wrong or what he was supposed to do next. Hugging the baby to his chest, he hopped frantically about his niche, his head swiveling around as if the answer was about to drop in on him from the sky. The baby's earsplitting cries joined in the swelling cacophony of shouts until the High Reaches, I'm sorry to say, was in a state of complete pandemonium. It was then, at the center of the storm, that Raphael figured out that Noble Tasks were maybe a little harder than he'd anticipated and that he'd better ask for help right away. He catapulted out of his niche straight for Madra-Dubh.

Madra-Dubh was doing his best to figure out what was going on when Raphael appeared next to him in a state of such extreme dishevelment that the gargoyle was taken aback. He gaped as Raphael thrust a small yowling bundle at him.

"Madra-Dubh," gasped the chimère, "how do I make it stop?!"

Madra-Dubh took a long look at the bundle. Very slowly he looked back up at Raphael. He opened his mouth. Nothing came out. He shut it and opened it again. This time it worked.

"Raphael," Madra-Dubh said. "Raphael, where did you *get that?*"

"The foundling box," wailed the chimère, pulling the red-faced howling baby back to his chest. "It's my Noble Task, I think—you see the monks can't—well, I thought— *MADRA-DUBH, YOU HAVE TO HELP ME!*"

At this, the gargoyle spat out an explosive burst of Gaelic (his carver had been a strapping young fellow named Conaill whose chisel slipped a lot), which, even if it were translatable at this late date, would nonetheless remain entirely unprintable. And the baby, having seen yet another remarkable face in what was working out to be a remarkable night, had somehow redoubled the volume of its screaming. Raphael was driven practically out of his mind. From the very depths of his being ripped the shriek, "Madra-Dubh, we have to do something!"

Raphael's desperate cry worked like a sharp slap; Madra-Dubh snapped right back into the cool shrewdness under fire for which gargoyles are justifiably renowned. "Hold on," he said grimly. "Think. Think. It's a baby. It needs baby things. SHUT UP! Who does babies? We don't do babies. Babies. FOR PITY'S SAKE, SHUT UP! Mice do babies! Pigeons do

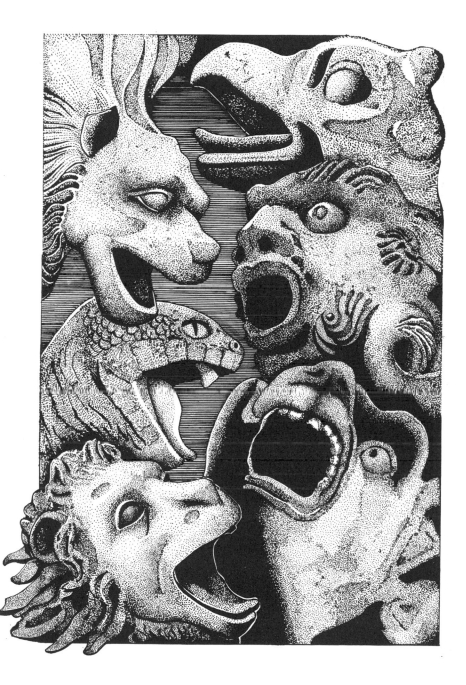

babies! Hold on to your flapping-eared face," Madra-Dubh cried triumphantly to Raphael, "I'm going to have to cry the Havoc!"

What happened next was something that hadn't happened in a hundred years. Yet no matter how much time may have passed, every gargoyle remembers the Havoc like you remember what to do when someone right next to you screams "Run!" As Madra-Dubh began the piercing howl that starts the Havoc, every gargoyle was struck instantaneously into shocked silence, but then the howl was taken up by every throat in every corner of the Cathedral, inside and out, until it seemed that the walls shook to the very foundations in the earth. This is the howl that means emergency, fire, turmoil, and flight, the howl that tells every nonhuman denizen of the Cathedral that the Cathedral is to stand to war. The howl split the sky for no more than a second before it stopped as sharply as if it had been sliced from the air. And in the beat of utter silence that followed, Madra-Dubh roared out, "MADRA-DUBH CALLS THE CONVOCATION ON THE HIGH REACHES! THE GENTLE ONES! THE GRAY-WINGS! TO *ME*!"

Chapter Eleven

Now it goes without saying that such a thunder, while intended to alert only the nonhuman residents of the Cathedral, would not go unremarked by the human ones as well. In the Cloister the monks sat bolt upright in their beds, their hearts pounding and their hair standing straight up. But it takes a moment for people to pass from sleep to wakefulness, and when their muzzy heads cleared, they heard nothing. Most of them, convinced it was only a nightmare that woke them, immediately turned over and went back to sleep. Several others ascribed their condition to the particularly awful quality of the beer at dinner that night and did the same. Even the Infirmarer's dog roused only briefly from his repose.

But Abbot Gregory remained vigilant. He knew that something extremely unusual had just occurred, even if he couldn't exactly identify what; so after a time of lying quietly in his bed, waiting to see if something equally dramatic followed that extraordinary sound, he decided to get up and take a look around.

If Abbot Gregory had been a little less tired and thus a little quicker on his feet, he would have reached the Cloister door in time to see a truly amazing sight. Across the icy garden of the Cloister dashed perfect flying phalanxes of mice, one after another, a show of precision that would put any of our army drills to shame. Overhead, from every direction, pigeons burst upwards from the rooftops of the houses and arrowed through the air straight for the High Reaches. This dramatic display passed so quickly, however, that by the time Abbot Gregory pushed open the heavy wooden door and stepped outside into the frozen night, all had once again fallen perfectly still.

First enormous rats, and now gigantic booms, thought the Abbot groggily. *I've definitely been working too hard. I've got to go to bed.*

Abbot Gregory would never have slept again had he seen what was happening up on the High Reaches. An astonishing convention gathered on the wide balcony behind Raphael's niche. First swarmed the mice, row after row of tiny gray bodies arranging themselves in ranks and clusters, according to which mouse society they belonged. Closest to the edge were the High Reaches mice, next to them the Cathedral propers; holding the center stood the Cloister, Dormitory, and Chapter House clans, and, to the right, the Yard and Granary societies, which were significantly more chaotic in their organization and caused not a small amount of fuss about placement. So many mice responded that they completely filled the balcony and overflowed down the walkways and the stairwells. Above them, dropping down from the sky like parachutists, the pigeons were landing upon every point and promontory available in a whirlwind of flapping wings and loose feathers. (Madra-Dubh himself had to swat away two or three of the less-respectful individuals.) And as each mouse and pigeon arriving had a great number of questions, the chittering and squawking were utterly deafening. This went on for a short time until Madra-Dubh, seeing that the quorum had assembled, decided that it was time to get things underway.

"Silence!" he shouted. "Madra-Dubh declares it is time for the Convocation to begin!"

The noise gradually died down as Madra-Dubh glared at each and every mouse and pigeon present to get his point across. But a small ripple had begun at the very center of the mouse clans. It grew until one could see that the mice were parting to each side to allow a very small, very old mouse passage through. The mouse limped haltingly forward, every eye fastened upon it, until it reached the small open space at the edge of the balcony. There it reared up on its hind legs and bowed gravely to Madra-Dubh. Madra-Dubh bowed just as seriously back to the mouse. You should not be surprised that Madra-Dubh had changed to such a courteous manner, despite his earlier vulgarity, because of all the gargoyles Madra-Dubh knew best how to conduct himself when serious matters were afoot.

The mouse declared in a piping yet authoritative voice, "The Mouse Societies greet the most excellent Madra-Dubh, Great Sentinel of the Cathedral Walls." (For that was indeed Madra-Dubh's title, though he would never mention it in ordinary conversation.) The mouse continued, "We have come, as is our duty, in response to your call. But on what ground does Madra-Dubh cry the Havoc and invoke the Convocation? We perceive no emergency requiring such drastic methods."

The challenge was quite serious, for this was Erian speaking, the venerable Great Elder of the Mouse Clans, a mouse so old and wise that each mouse society had agreed she would speak for all as long as she lived. Madra-Dubh knew that his response to Erian's pointed question might determine the outcome of the entire Convocation. Mice put great weight in the opinions of their elders, and were Erian to reject his need for help, then it was likely that the other mice would follow. The pigeons, being, well, birdbrains, would certainly mirror the mice in their decision without a second thought. It was a critical moment, and yet Madra-Dubh said nothing. He merely nodded his head sharply at a shadow huddled overlooked against the wall.

There was a pause, and then Raphael stepped hesitantly forward into the moonlight. He was very careful to watch where he put his feet. Cradled in one arm he held the bundled-up baby, now silent. For, in the manner of babies, it had wailed until it had wailed enough to express its displeasure and then it had fallen asleep. Madra-Dubh let the assemblage take a good long look at Raphael before he spoke. "This is the ground upon which I dared cry the Havoc," he declared.

"It's a chimère, that's all it is," cried one puzzled voice from over near the stairwell.

"What's it got with it?" burbled a pigeon overhead. And then everyone started talking again so that no one could hear themselves think.

In the hubbub, Erian looked steadily at Raphael, then nodded as if she'd just become certain of something. "Most honorable Raphael," she said gently. "For what great need, young Guardian, have you got us all up in the middle of the night?"

Raphael cast a pleading glance up at Madra-Dubh, who inclined his head in response. Raphael carefully unwrapped the cloth. The entire Convocation gasped as one when they saw the baby, pink and warm, its eyes squeezed shut as it slept with all its might. Even Erian, who, as Great Elder, was mostly immune to surprises, had to sit down for this revelation. From the prominences and promontories all around came a fury of flapping as pigeons burst into the air. They had

to circle frenziedly for a while until they could calm themselves down enough to land again. In the center of it all stood
Raphael, quivering noticeably with anxiety, and Madra-
Dubh, who was rather better at hiding it and so looked more
composed.

When things had quieted down again, Erian, trying to
conceal her amazement with her enormous dignity, said to
Raphael, "How come you to have a human child?"

Raphael steeled himself. "I think it's my Noble Task," he
said simply. Again the balcony erupted into chaos. Cries of
"Noble what?" and "Get on!" could be clearly discerned amid
the babble. Erian made a sharp movement with one of her
paws, and the hubbub abruptly ceased, except for the tiny
voice of one very young mouse imploring, "What's a Noble
Task, Momma?"

Erian sighed. "Perhaps you'd better explain this to us,
Raphael," she said kindly, even though an old Cathedral leg-
end told her exactly what Raphael meant. (You will hear that
story too, as Raphael does, when the time is right.) And so
Raphael explained at length to that dubious gathering the
sense of loneliness that drove him to the Alchemist, and
what the Alchemist said about Raphael's need for a Noble
Task; his encounters with the tomb effigies, and then with
the gargoyles (Erian cut her eyes over to Madra-Dubh during
this part, who nodded ever so slightly as Raphael spoke);
and, finally, of his journey to the Scriptorium, and the books'

refusal to speak. He hesitated here, waiting for the Convocation's indignant response to his presumption. But aside from a few puzzled mutterings they remained quiet, so he drove on with increasing confidence. He told about seeing the young woman on the steps and his shattering realization that caring for the baby she left behind might, at last, be his Noble Task. Once he finished telling about the woman, he remembered that he'd forgotten one very important part—his discovery of the picture of the Silver Knight and the evil dragon, the terrifying visit of the Silver Knight to the Cathedral, and Raphael's belief that caring for the baby might protect him from the Knight—but, as he told himself, explaining *everything* might just complicate matters. So he skipped that part and went on, feeling a little ashamed of his secret reason for taking the baby, but even more ashamed to admit his weakness to the entire Cathedral.

When he finished his story, the balcony was completely hushed. Erian was deep in thought. Madra-Dubh's expression was grave. Raphael sat motionless in the center, cradling the sleeping baby. At last Erian spoke.

"We all have tasks at the Cathedral," the old mouse said slowly. "All of us, from the greatest Sentinel"—here she bowed to Madra-Dubh—"to the smallest mouse and pigeon, all have a role we must fulfill. The Sentinels watch and warn; the chimères greet and guard; the effigies and sculptures remind us of the ones we are to respect and remember; the pigeons are the eyes and ears; the mice protect and teach our tradition. The monks themselves have their own role, and it does not intersect with ours; for as it is said,

> *Let not the way of mouse and stone*
> *Take traverse that is man's alone.*

That is the plan our great Architect wrought, and that is how it has always been."

The Convocation murmured as one in agreement. Every mouse pup and pigeon chick, every gargoyle and chimère, were taught these words before any other. They were the First Rule of the Cathedral, and they might as well have been engraved in the stone itself. A heavy silence fell again.

Erian's voice rang across the balcony like a small piercing bell. "You must give the baby to the monks, Raphael. That is the Rule we must follow."

Raphael's response was immediate. It was also unexpected. He clutched the sleeping baby closer to himself and said, "No."

There was a moment of stillness as the shock of Raphael's refusal of the Great Elder sank into the multitude. Even the wearying wind halted. The world seemed struck voiceless. Through the clouds the stars alone keened in the night, and from the sky close overhead the first flakes of snow touched the Convocation. Into this hush Raphael repeated bravely, as if they hadn't heard him the first time: "No, I won't."

"You—*won't?!*" shrieked a pigeon, for pigeons are very good at shrieking, and, once somebody had said something, everyone had to join in with their opinion, and there arose from the High Reaches that instant a clamor so extraordinary that all of the hubbubs before it seemed like mere rehearsals. In fact, Madra-Dubh was hard-pressed to stop it from becoming another Havoc. By virtue of a great deal of flailing around he managed to get everyone's attention briefly just as Erian shouted at Raphael, "How dare you reject the word of the Elders!"

"Because the monks have no food!" Raphael shouted back. His wings had flared out without thought and his tail lashed about his legs. He looked enormous and fierce and, to speak quite honestly, terrifying—if he had been able to see himself, he would no longer have had any doubt about his fitness to defend the Cathedral—and around him the mice shrank back against the walls and the pigeons fled in flight to higher promontories. Yet, within the safety of his arms, the baby slept on unconcerned.

"Is this true?" Erian snapped at the Dormitory and Granary mice. "Is there no food?"

The august elders of those mouse societies chattered amongst themselves in total disarray. Finally one of the Yard mice, disgusted, stepped forward (while casting a wary eye on Raphael, who was still in full defensive posture) to say, "He speaks rightly, th'young Guardian—there is very little, and that's full of weevils and rot, truly said."

"There must be some excess to feed something so small," a pigeon bleated from a cautious distance.

"I heard one of the monks speak in the Scriptorium," Raphael shot back. He'd folded his wings in embarrassment at his earlier excess of emotion, but his voice was still insistent. "The monk said that there was no food to give another baby. There might be enough, if *we* do it, but that's what the human said: 'If one more child is abandoned here, I will have nothing to give it.' How can I give the baby to the monks, if they will only let it starve? Is that what the First Rule means?"

The chimère and the elder mouse glared at each other until Erian sighed and sat down. Madra-Dubh rubbed his eyes, which were intended to search far horizons, not study tiny gray furry things boiling around practically underfoot. Nothing like this had ever happened before at the Cathedral, and all were without guideposts, without moorings; and perhaps it is a sign of the gallantry of these small creatures in the face of an undiscovered country that Erian said at last, without rancor, "This is your Noble Task, then. We will help you."

This deliverance made Raphael gasp. His heart skipped again, though, when Erian added, "But there are conditions.

If food comes—or if the baby's mother comes—then you must give the baby back."

Raphael nodded gravely, and Erian bowed deeply to him. It was at this wordless sign that the Convocation began to trickle away, down the steps and through the air. Left behind were Erian, Madra-Dubh, a small circle of mouse scholars, and Raphael, cradling a sleeping baby and shuddering with a relief so sharp he feared he would weep.

Chapter Twelve

hat followed then was the most extraordinary time in the life of the Cathedral. Whereas before the mice, the pigeons, and the gargoyles and chimères had existed in completely different spheres, each living only within his own narrow community, now that the baby had come they worked together as smoothly as if such cooperation had been intended all along.

The mouse council of scholars coordinated the supply lines, directing each mouse society to find such necessary provisions as the baby required. Thus, the Dormitory and Cloister mice searched through the monks' linens to find blankets, cloths, and parchment that could be twisted into paps (like our rubber nipples, but not quite as reliable) from which the baby could nurse. They also ran shifts all night long before the banked fire in the Scriptorium, warming wrapping cloths, which the pigeons would then whisk up to the baby. The Yard mice spirited away small crockery bottles (originally intended for the Infirmarer's herbal tinctures) from the Potter's shed to hold the baby's milk. And the Granary and Kitchen mice scoured the pantries for porridge and mashed vegetables (originally intended by the Abbey Cook for the older and largely toothless dwellers of the monastery) to carry up to the High Reaches for the baby's feedings. Each item was laboriously transported in tiny increments from mouse to mouse or with the help of pigeons under the very noses of the monks and Cathedral visitors. There was only one problem: no matter what container they found or what strategy they tried, the mice and pigeons could not come up with a method to get milk to Raphael's niche. Even the little crockery bottles were too heavy to carry very far at all when filled, and any other container merely spilled the precious fluid. Though the mice and pigeons tried for two days to come up with a solution, there was no helping it; the task simply couldn't be done.

Up on the High Reaches, while Raphael carefully gathered clean meltwater from the snowy rooflines to satisfy the baby's thirst, Erian and Madra-Dubh racked their brains for hours. It was evident that while there would be enough food, the baby still required milk to be well. It was left to Raphael, the youngest and least experienced of all of them, to arrive at the answer.

"Well, if we can't bring the cow to the baby," Raphael said, "why can't we bring the baby to the cow?"

Erian and Madra-Dubh stared at him. A chimère, leaving the Cathedral? Such a thing was without precedent! Incomprehensible! Completely, absolutely, and totally—

"Sensible," Madra-Dubh finally grumbled, shaking his head at Erian. "Now why didn't *you* think of that?"

"Because it's impossible!" snapped Erian ferociously. "The Architect would never have dreamed of such a thing!"

"Well, *pickle* me if there aren't a *passel* of things that the Architect forgot to dream about!" Madra-Dubh retorted, pointing dramatically over at the baby. A goofily grinning Raphael was playing clawsies with it as it giggled and batted at the chimère's dancing paws. The gargoyle sighed, clutching his head. "We're muzzle-deep in this mess already, Erian, and there's nothing else to do about it, Architect or no Architect, who, I may point out, is Not—Here—Anyway."

Erian glared at the huddle of mouse scholars on the balcony. They shrugged sheepishly back at her. Nothing in the entire history of the Cathedral's mouse texts seemed to say anything about caring for human babies, though teams of elders were poring over every document written by a mouse since the founding of the Abbey. Instead, they'd been forced to cobble together bits and pieces of information from what

mice and pigeons did for their own babies, supplemented by what the occasional mouse had seen humans do. (As it happened, everyone had overlooked something you or I would find quite important—the need for diapers, and someone to change them regularly. This oversight caused no small amount of consternation and generalized running about on the High Reaches when the inevitable event occurred for the first time.) Erian knew she had no choice but to agree to Raphael's idea, but she was at a loss for practical suggestions. It certainly looked like the only way to get milk for the baby would be to have Raphael carry it off the Cathedral and to the cows in the Yard far below. But how to do this? The problem seemed insurmountable.

"The baby will fall off as you climb down the walls," she protested. "Coming *up* is one thing, but you need all four feet to make the journey *down,* don't you?"

"Oh dear," said Raphael. He thought as hard as he could, but he had to admit that Erian was right. All three of them—Elder Mouse, gargoyle, and chimère—stared disconsolately out over the Cathedral Square. A cart groaned and shuddered its way across the cobbles, pulled in a most unwilling fashion by a flop-eared, low-headed horse of unfortunate proportions. Something tickled at Madra-Dubh as he watched the cob hitch irregularly along. When the nag shook its head with irritation, jangling the buckles on its harness, a great light suddenly went on inside Madra-Dubh's head and he cried, "A harness! Blast us all for pimple-headed nitwits, we'll strap the baby on with a *harness!*"

Immediately a pigeon was called to take a message to the Yard mice, and for a few hours after that the nooks and corners of the Yard boiled with activity. The Stable subclan of the Yard mouse society was delighted to assist. They were the handiest mice of all, and there was usually not much demand for their skills in the regular life of the Cathedral. With delight they rose to the occasion. It did not take long before they had fashioned a quite suitable harness from a small wicker basket, lined with a cleverly trimmed sheepskin saddle pad for the baby, all held securely atop Raphael's back with bridle straps and girth buckles painstakingly scavenged from the Abbey's tack supplies. With the Yard cows having been persuaded at some length to assist in the task (the cows, being somewhat slow-witted, were not immediately enthusiastic about the prospect of a dragon-headed, eagle-winged griffin poking about their pen, baby or no baby), all that was left to do was wait for darkness to fall.

When finally the sun had set, Raphael and the mice carefully lifted the baby into the basket and cinched down the loose-woven wicker lid. Inside, the baby cooed and giggled delightedly, as it had decided, in the manner of babies, that since it had a full belly and plenty of attention from the interesting-looking creatures caring for it, all was well. Madra-Dubh, Erian, and the mice wished Raphael good luck. With their hearts in their throats, they watched as

Raphael cautiously crept from his niche and scaled down the West Façade. Ledge to ledge, lintel to lintel, Raphael slowly descended, accompanied by a worried flurry of pigeons circling close overhead, shouting well-meaning but essentially useless advice. Atop Raphael's back the basket swayed but did not slip. At last Raphael leapt lightly from the last outcrop and sighed hugely as his claws clacked on the cobblestones of the Square. He was safely down.

Far away up on the High Reaches a pandemonium erupted, equal parts joy and relief. The pigeons headed back to those lofty heights, congratulating themselves as they flew for their wisdom, as if they'd accomplished the amazing feat themselves. Raphael gave them all a quick wave and immediately turned to his goal. With the map of the Yard clear in his head (earlier that evening, the leader of the Yard mice had tutored Raphael on this over and over again), he negotiated his way along the side of the Cathedral, around the manure pile, and past the Baker's hut, arrowing straight for the cowshed on the far side of the Yard.

To anyone watching, which there shouldn't have been at that hour, he would have been only an uncertain shadow among shadows. Most people, you and I included, would have simply rubbed our eyes and gone to bed. But Goody Baker was another sort of person entirely. Sitting grumpily on the ground before her rather nice little hut, she was contemplating the slights and insults that she believed other people had given her during that day, and the day before, and for quite some time before that. So she was wide awake when she saw a slender, flare-winged shadow hesitate at the corner of the Yard, twitch itself as if to adjust something, and then sprint headlong through the moonlight until it disappeared into the yawning darkness of the cowshed.

Chapter Thirteen

Goody Baker got up, brushed off her skirt, and went inside to get her broom.

Inside the engulfing blackness of the cowshed Raphael searched desperately for something to orient himself. There was only a regular munching sound, an occasional blubbering sigh, and the creak of shifting weight on wood in the warm darkness. It seemed an eternity before a tiny chiming voice directly at his left ear made him jump. "So it's you, guv'nor," said a mouse. "You'd think you'd swum from Araby for all this time waiting. Come on, now, we're all ready for you."

Now Raphael could see a swarm of mice boiling up to him from all directions, appearing in the hay shoved in great leaning piles in the corners, and from every crack and cranny in the wooden floor and walls. They vaulted atop him without hesitation and started to work on the buckles of the wicker basket. In only a moment they had the lid off on one side and were busily handing the tiny crockery bottles, packed carefully around the baby, down a living chain of mice. Each bottle was then spirited away into the darkness. As Raphael's eyes adjusted, he could see that each bottle was taken to a cow tied to a manger, and that a crew of three mice then worked to fill the bottle: one holding the bottle straight, and two tugging on a teat of the cow's udder to fill the crockery with streams of steaming white milk.

"You might want to take the wee 'un to Roses, right before you," remarked the sweet treble voice again. It belonged to a particularly large mouse who was now unconcernedly cleaning his whiskers inches from Raphael's teeth (a certain audacity being an important part of Stable mouse attitude). "Cooperative old sort, that Roses, a real dear." When Raphael didn't move but simply looked puzzled, the Stable watchmouse repeated slowly and clearly, as one might speak to an infant, "Take the baby to the cow and let 'im nurse awhile, guv'nor. That's it."

Raphael hesitantly approached the nearest cow. She was lying on her side, her jaw moving rhythmically, eyeing Raphael with some suspicion. But she did not protest as Raphael reached behind himself and took the baby from the basket to show her. She examined the baby closely, snuffled briefly at it, then nodded. (Cows don't speak much because words take up space better filled with food.) With some tartly offered assistance from the Stable watchmouse,

Raphael positioned the baby at the cow's udder and stepped back. The baby went to work with a will. There followed a time of quiet as the baby nursed, the mice finished their work, and Raphael took the corked bottles from them one by one and put them back in his harness basket.

Into this happy peace, as was her usual *modus operandi*, stormed an enraged Goody Baker.

The goodwife had armed herself with her biggest broom and a tallow candle, as if she were a knight heading for the Crusades, and marched without hesitation straight to the cowshed. Those were her cows, by St. Bertha, and nothing—not even a useless drunken husband snoring in the face of peril—was going to stop her from defending them from . . . well . . . whatever it was that went in there! She squared her robust frame and tore the door open, thrusting the candle inside as she shouted, "Got you!"

What Goody saw was Raphael, wide-eyed in the glare for a split second before he simply vanished. Goody shrieked and waded into the cowshed swinging her broom wildly, but Raphael was gone. In that instant he'd grabbed the baby and bounded straight up into the air, where he scrambled onto a rafter overhead, every scale standing on end and his tail puffed out to the size of a sofa bolster. The baby was struck silent with shock for a moment, having its dinner so rudely interrupted, but then opened its mouth and sucked in an alarming lungful of air. From his experience on the High Reaches, Raphael knew exactly what was going to happen next. He grabbed a full bottle from his basket, dipped in a claw, and poked the claw into the baby's gaping mouth.

The baby quieted instantly and set about contented sucking. Raphael feverishly dipped every claw he had into the bottle and there followed a frenzied round of claw-swapping as the baby went through each in turn. But at least there was no sound. Raphael huddled up as small as possible on the rafter and wished fervently for the human below to go away. As he shifted himself, a little crockery bottle teetered perilously on the edge of the opened basket on his back.

Now, Goody Baker thought herself no fool. She'd seen something, all right, and she was going to find it. She carefully paced the perimeter of the cowshed, squinting narrow-eyed into every nook and corner, brandishing her candle at anything that looked suspicious. But as she was not a particularly inventive person, it never occurred to her to look overhead; and so she saw nothing except the cows, who stared back at her with their usual bland expressions. Nothing moved except the steady bovine jaws.

Goody Baker was nonplussed. Maybe whatever it was had gone. Maybe she should go to bed.

This, of course, was when the small crockery bottle in Raphael's harness basket finally tipped over and fell. Raphael and the mice watched in horror as it tumbled gracefully through the air and landed with a little clunk in the hay directly between Goody Baker's feet.

Goody Baker grunted in confusion and bent down to examine it.

The Stable watchmouse was clinging to the wall directly behind Goody Baker. Seeing this, he said "Ah, bloody 'ell!" in a disgusted sort of voice and jumped.

Now if you were standing alone in a very dark room, thinking that there might be something perfectly awful hidden somewhere inside it, you would probably do the same thing that Goody Baker did if a small, warm, furry thing suddenly thumped into your hair. She leapt straight up, and flung her arms in several different directions, and ran straight forward into the wall, shrieking "Aieeee!" The broom flew one way, the candle another, as Goody Baker bounced off the wall and began running in small circles beating frantically at her head. The Stable watchmouse had a blistering time of it trying to dodge her frenzied blows—he wasn't entirely successful, unfortunately—but in between poundings he managed to gasp out to Raphael, "Run, will you!"

Raphael tucked the baby under one arm and fled for his life. Halfway through the Yard he skidded to a halt and stuffed the wailing baby back into the basket, cinching down the lid as best he could before sprinting off again. All around him candles flared as people, jolted awake by Goody Baker's screams, tumbled from their doorways tugging on clothes and shouting. Through this pandemonium the chimère dashed with only one thought in mind—to get to the Cathedral and his safe niche on the West Façade.

Perhaps it was his fright that made him less careful than he should have been. Certainly it is unkind of us to judge him at this point; but the fact remains that several people, including some individuals widely regarded for their sobriety and sense, saw what they truly believed was a giant rat—a giant rat with a *saddle* on—maybe an imp, no, a demon—a demon the size of a cart horse with glowing red eyes breathing fire and enormous batlike wings, spurred on by the screaming spawn of Satan—racing like the fires of Hell itself for the walls of the Cathedral, where it vaulted up the stone and simply disappeared.

It wasn't long after Abbot Gregory got up the next morning that he began wishing he'd stayed in bed.

First of all, there had been the brouhaha the night before in the Yard, which had woken everyone up for no reason whatsoever except the foolishness of Goody Baker. It was a gift from God that the cowshed hadn't burned down, what with the woman bringing a lit candle into a wooden building full of dry hay. Her hysterical explanation of a giant demon bouncing around on top of her pate had given Gregory a splitting headache. It hadn't been helped, either, by the insistence of several people not ordinarily given to hallucinations that they too had seen the demon, and that it had headed straight for the Cathedral when they'd chased it.

And now this morning, with its long line of petitioners outside his chamber door. First was the Cellarer, who complained at length of unusual mouse activity in the storehouses for the last two days. Abbot Gregory tried to explain that of course there would be a lot of mice about, they hadn't any food either, and had he tried bringing the Infirmarer's dog Æthelred in to try to clean them out a bit? The Cellarer had acquiesced to the Abbot's suggestion rather too sullenly, but at least he'd gone away. The Potter who'd come in next was almost completely irrational, insisting that imps had been ransacking his stocks of tincture bottles, and demanding to know when was the Abbot going to send someone over for an exorcism. Abbot Gregory tried to explain that it was highly unlikely that imps would be interested in tincture bottles in the first place and secondly that exorcisms were usually intended for people, not pottery sheds. He'd practically had to escort the man forcibly out the door to get him to leave. Barely had his threshold been cleared before the Cook was in it, purple-faced with rage, shouting about missing mush portions, and then the Sacristan shouldered his way in to bellow incoherently about cloths disappearing, and then the Head Librarian showed up with a long-winded story about parchment supplies dwindling, and all of them repeating insistently: What was the Abbot going to do about it?

Quit and join the Franciscans, Abbot Gregory groaned to himself when he was finally alone. *Wandering without care on the roads and paths, nothing to my name but sandals and a robe, depending on the kindness of others to feed me. Besides, I'd look good in brown.*

But in fact Abbot Gregory was a very responsible man, and he well knew that he could not run away from his obligations. Especially as this day was Christmas Eve, and the Cathedral had to finish its preparations for one of the biggest celebrations of the year: the Midnight Mass, where the Church and its people would welcome the coming of a very important baby to the world. It was Gregory's favorite time of the year, but the groundwork boggled the mind. The new music that the head chorister was so wild about was still baffling the monks. The novices and small students had to have their parts in the Nativity mystery play practically pounded into their heads. The parishioners' procession had to be reorganized so what happened last year wouldn't happen again. (Gregory winced thinking about how much it had cost to replace the windows.) The decorations had to be completed, the Yule log wasn't here yet from the forests, the feast (though truly it would be a meager one this season unless the foresters got lucky) cooked and laid out. And none of this seemed to get done without Abbot Gregory's detailed and personal guidance. It was enough to drive anyone to distraction.

But as there was nothing to be done about it, Abbot Gregory sighed and walked resignedly out of his chamber to face the chaos. As soon as he entered the Cathedral he was immediately set upon by a swarm of little boys insisting that he watch them reenact Joseph and Mary's search for a place at the inn. And in no time at all, delighted by his students' exuberantly disorganized version of the old story (there were at least three Josephs, for example, and the innkeeper's dialogue was a lot saltier than he would have liked), Father Gregory completely forgot the reports of the mysterious events at the Cathedral.

Up on the High Reaches, however, those mysterious events continued unabated. Raphael was trying once again to explain to a livid Madra-Dubh exactly how things had gone so terribly wrong in the cowshed. Erian was consulting with the mouse scholars on what to do next, as most of the milk bottles in Raphael's basket had been lost during his flight. The conclusion that both Madra-Dubh and Erian were reaching was one that Raphael did not want to hear: the baby had to be returned to the monks.

"You can't be dragging the baby all over Creation," Madra-Dubh said heatedly to Raphael, who looked both abashed and protective of the baby cuddled in his arms. "They'll *see* you. They *saw* you! The whole suffering lot of them will be up here with *pitchforks!*" At this appalling thought Madra-Dubh had to stop to clutch his head with dismay. "Why is this happening to me? Do you have any understanding of what is going to happen here? Raphael, you have to give the baby back!"

"The milk won't last another day," Erian pronounced from the back of the balcony. "And you can't go down there again. There's no other choice, Raphael."

"But those aren't the only cows," protested Raphael. "I could take the baby to the fields, couldn't I? Nobody will see me this time, I promise."

Erian and Madra-Dubh started talking at the same time, but Raphael turned obstinately away and refused to listen. His conscience told him that what the Elders were saying was the right course. Keeping the baby would put his friends— perhaps even the Cathedral itself—in danger, if what Madra-Dubh had said was true. And with the milk running low, the baby would face starvation in time anyway. But the last two days had been so marvelous that the thought of leaving the baby with the monks tore at Raphael's heart. As it happened, Raphael was a very good nanny; he didn't need to sleep, and he had a virtually endless patience developed from many seasons of solitary guard duty in often difficult circumstances. During the baby's fussy times he told long stories about the Cathedral; when the baby slept at last, he cradled the little warm bundle to his chest as he watched over the Square. The baby thrived in his gentle care, and a thriving baby is very good company indeed. There had been many moments when Raphael had thought he would burst with happiness. To voluntarily end that happiness—to return to loneliness, to despair—the thought was intolerable.

So Raphael ignored the small voice of his conscience and chose instead to fight with Madra-Dubh and Erian. The discussion became so heated that the noise woke up the baby nestled in Raphael's arms. Raphael automatically began rocking it in the practiced way he'd developed over the last two nights, and the baby grudgingly subsided back into sleep, but not before a few wails had echoed across the High Reaches, down the left hand spiral staircase, and into the ears of a certain monk named Brother John.

Brother John was very sad that morning. He was sitting on the lower steps of the staircase crying a little because Brother Michael had snapped at him for polishing a statue wrong and had sent him away to "bother someone else." Even though Brother John was all grown up, you see, he was still a little boy inside, and sometimes things that came easily to the other monks were very hard for him. He loved the Cathedral and the monks and Abbot Gregory most of all, because the Abbot had taken him in when no one else wanted him, and it frustrated him terribly when he couldn't help the way he wanted to. In times like that he would usually go see Gregory, and Gregory would make him feel better. But today the Abbot was terribly busy, so Brother John had run away to hide in the spiral staircase.

When the wailing sounds first reached him, Brother John thought he was hearing himself cry; but soon he realized that it wasn't him at all. It was a baby. Curious, he stopped snuffling and wiped his runny nose on his robe. Yes, it was a baby, and it was somewhere upstairs. Brother John started up the steps to look at it, but remembered that Abbot Gregory had told him that he was never, ever to go up there by himself because he could fall. So he decided instead to go tell Abbot Gregory and went to find him in the Cathedral.

At any other time, Abbot Gregory would have sat down with Brother John and listened to him very carefully. But today, as we know, he was doing fifteen different things at once, all of which were critically important to the people speaking at him from every direction. So when Brother John tugged at his robe, we should perhaps forgive Gregory for being a bit distracted.

"Baby up there," Brother John said.

Abbot Gregory said, "Hmm?", trying to listen to John as well as study the music that Brother Brian, the Chorister, was flapping vigorously in front of his face. Brother John tugged at Gregory's sleeve again. "Baby up there," he repeated, pointing vaguely up at the ceiling.

Abbot Gregory finally looked at John and followed the monk's finger up to the fan vaults. "Oh," he agreed absently, "yes. Baby Jesus up there. Tomorrow is Christmas Day, John, when the baby Jesus came down to be with us." He returned his attention to the music and Brother Brian's frantic importunings.

Brother John's face clouded with confusion and then cleared into an expression of pure delight. "Baby Jesus coming tomorrow!" he exclaimed. "Baby Jesus coming!" He dashed off to the Kitchen to tell the Cook, who would usually give John a little something to eat whenever he brought interesting news.

Brother John was to be disappointed at first, because the Cook was busy too, but it was a very joyful kind of business. He was standing bare-armed in the middle of the Kitchen Yard without the cold wind bothering him in the least, because he was working very hard: Nicholas of Bedford's wagon train full of food had just arrived, and he was helping unload pack after pack of meat and vegetables, and shocks of grain, and casks of wine and beer. The sheer abundance of it all had the Cook close to tears. Not an hour ago he had been at his wits' end, trying to figure out how to turn moldy turnips, and weevily corn, and a few shriveled apples into a proper Christmas feast, and now this! From his lips sprang a completely spontaneous (although utterly tuneless) song of thanksgiving. When Brother John came up to him pointing at the Cathedral rooftop and babbling excitedly about the Baby Jesus coming, the Cook beamed widely, said "Praise God, that's the truth," gave John an enormous hug and told him to go find the Cellarer right away.

Brother John gestured at a basket of parsnips going by on a grimacing servant's back. "But Baby Jesus needs dinner," he

said helpfully and made to snatch one. The Cook stopped
him. "God takes care of the Baby Jesus," he assured the monk
solemnly, nabbing a little bun from another basket and pressing it into the open hand. "Cook takes care of Brother John.
Now run along and find Brother Mark. We've got a lot of
wine to unload!"

Brother John dashed for the Cathedral, his cheeks
bulging with bread. As he ran, he narrowly missed trampling
a small, fragile figure hesitantly weaving its way through the
madness of the Kitchen Yard. It was a young woman dressed
in black—the same young woman we've met before, on the
cold night steps of the Cathedral—but now her back was
straight and her face was lit with joy. Juliana had kept her
promise. She was coming back for her baby.

Chapter Fifteen

Nicholas of Bedford's caravan had brought more than food, you see; it also had brought news from the villages and manors along its route. In one of those villages an old couple had paid the local priest to scribe a letter to their widowed daughter, asking her to come home with her baby. They wrote that they had found steady work as servants in the local lord's manor and now there was enough food for everyone. The priest had taken the letter to Nicholas when the young merchant's caravan stopped for the night, and Nicholas had agreed to take the letter to the town. He refused the priest's offer of payment, for he had suffered a terrible loss himself not long ago, and it warmed his heart to be the bearer of good news. Not to mention the fact that he anticipated making quite a nice profit on this trip and the priest's coin would be better spent buying the services of a laundress for his ghastly robe.

When Nicholas's wagons finally reached the town, he dispatched one of his guards to take the letter to the address printed laboriously on it, and promptly forgot the whole matter. It was unfortunate that he didn't go himself, because then he would have seen one of the great sights that humans are fortunate to experience: the vision of a desperate and despairing person receiving help when it seemed all hope was lost. Juliana tore the letter open with trembling hands as she raced downstairs to the leather merchant in the shopfront below her cold, empty little room. The leather merchant did not at first wish to help her—he was a very busy man—but something about the expression on Juliana's face softened his heart, and he muddled through the crabbed handwriting well enough in the end. In fact, when Juliana left, the merchant was whistling like the King's own minstrel. It's odd how even someone else's good news can lift a person's spirits. It also didn't hurt that the grateful kiss he'd gotten from an overjoyed Juliana had been the best thing to happen to him since his shrewish wife ran away with the tinsmith.

Juliana wasted no time after hearing the good news. She dashed about packing her few things into a single bag and then clattered down the rickety steps to the street, her mind fixed only on the Cathedral and her baby. She felt no regret leaving behind the little room that she and her husband, Joseph, had worked so hard to afford. After his death in an accident, she had been forced to sell, piece by piece, all of their possessions simply to buy food for herself and her little son. Eventually there had been nothing left to sell, and that was when she left her baby in the foundling box. Though she was terribly weak and ill from hunger, the letter's promise had filled her with a new strength. When she raced down the street she felt as if she were flying.

Now, staring wide-eyed at the confusion swirling about her in the Cathedral, she hardly knew what to do. She tried to gain the attention of the monks whisking past her, but they all shook their heads brusquely and continued on. Eventually she found one, staring a bit befuddled at an odd piece of parchment in his hand, who actually answered her when she spoke to him.

"Please, Father, I've come back for my baby," she told the monk.

Few words could have been more surprising to Abbot Gregory. He tucked the music sheet under one arm and studied the frail young woman standing a little unsteadily before him. He looked closely at her face, noting thoughtfully the tight draw of little food, the two bright spots of fever in her cheeks. "Young widow," he said respectfully, "of a baby I know nothing. Surely I have misunderstood?"

What happened next was so startling that it even caught the attention of a Cathedral proper mouse, who, as is the way of the proper mice, had developed a certain obliviousness to the antics of the monks and visitors inside. The mouse in question had been nosing about in a thicket of stone flowers about halfway up the Nave wall when she heard a terrible, gasping cry. Startled, the mouse looked up to see a woman dashing headlong for the Great Portal, stumbling and falling, and a monk—the Elder Personage, in fact— catching her as she plunged to the stone. The Elder Personage lifted the woman in his arms and, as monks scattered everywhere around him, their robes flying in disarray, headed at a good pace for the door into the Cloister.

This was by far the most unusual event that the Cathedral proper mouse had seen since the Convocation not three days ago and deserved some following-up. She hopped neatly from stone to stone until she was well positioned above the door to the Cloister and craned her head as the Elder Personage whisked by, carrying the woman. So she heard the Elder Personage shout to another monk, "She's ill—Infirmary—" and the woman moan, "Please, I've lost—" before the door banged shut behind them.

Without hesitation the mouse turned and raced straight up the wall for the Clerestory. She knew that something important was happening, although exactly what it was she could not yet tell, and this meant that the news must be passed at once. Through one of the small Clerestory windows (which were clear glass, as they were intended only to admit light into the Cathedral) the mouse signaled frantically to a pigeon outside. It stopped cleaning its feathers and stared at her with a shocked expression.

"Something's happened," the mouse shouted. "Bear news to the Dormitory watchmice to stand guard in the Infirmary! Notify the elder mice! Go now!"

When clearly and specifically instructed, a pigeon will generally do what you tell it. The bird exploded into flight and headed straight for the Dormitory, where it circled overhead, shrieking an alarm so annoying that one of the students threw a rock at it. It also got the attention of the watchmice on the roofs, who managed to get the pigeon to land and extracted the Cathedral proper's message from it. (This took quite a bit of persuasion, as the pigeon kept babbling hysterically about big rocks and little boys.) The bravest among the watchmice ran immediately for the Infirmary. He arrived at the door just as Abbot Gregory ducked inside the threshold with the woman. As he was a very practical mouse, he used the Abbot's own robe to conceal himself as he dashed across the floor and hid in the rushes beneath the bed.

The hay-filled mattress above his head groaned and settled as the Abbot carefully placed Juliana on it. The watchmouse heard the young woman tossing restlessly, crying out, "You must have him. I left him here, in the foundling box! Please, I've lost my baby," and the Elder Personage murmuring, "All will be right. I promise, it will be set right."

The watchmouse was electrified. A *baby!* The woman was speaking of a *baby!* Watchmice are not stupid creatures and, true to form, this one immediately figured out that the woman was the mother of the baby in the High Reaches. All of his fur puffed up and his whiskers bristled with the sheer emergency of the situation. Erian must be told at once. The baby must be returned. He must run for the High Reaches right away!

The watchmouse had raced nearly halfway across the floor when he remembered something very important.

He was in the Infirmary.

The Infirmarer had a ferocious dog.

And now they both had arrived.

Chapter Sixteen

eanwhile, up on the High Reaches, things were becoming very busy. For an hour or so, pigeons had been dropping to the balcony to report many horses and wagons and humans in the Kitchen Yard. Erian had despaired over making any sense out of them, for the pigeons were extremely excited and had a tendency to fly away in midsentence. Eventually Madra-Dubh had to take a chance and start an All's-Well among the gargoyles to find out what was going on, even though it was still daylight and there were many people about.

Raphael quietly played with the baby as they all waited for the All's-Well to return. He had just fed the little boy a tiny pot of soft-cooked parsnips, offered one by one on the very tip of Raphael's claw. The baby had eaten all of it, cooing with delight, and had then started batting at Raphael's paws. Raphael found himself laughing almost immediately.

He was grateful for any distraction, as in the corner of his eye he could see the very last bottle of milk sitting by itself on the edge of the balcony. Once that was gone, his joy would surely come to an end, unless he could think of an alternative at once.

There must be something I could do, he fretted to himself. *Madra-Dubh and Erian say I must give the baby back, but they can't make me, can they? Especially because the monks still have no food. There's no rule saying I have to take him back. I love him.* He seized the baby tightly to his chest and hugged him. The baby laughed, his very first real laugh, and Raphael thought his heart would break in two.

From over on the far side of the balcony, Erian shouted, "The All's-Well is coming in!"

Raphael trembled in the moment of silence that followed. From a few buttresses over finally came the expected chorus, but almost hissed this time, as Madra-Dubh had made some enormously creative threats about what would happen if the gargoyles didn't keep the noise down: "ALL'S WELL ON THE SOUTH NAVE, AND THERE'S A PILE OF FOOD ARRIVED IN THE KITCHEN YARD FOR SUCH AS EATS IT, YOU QUEASY BESLUBBERING SHEEP-BITING PUMPIONS."

"That's the South Nave all right," Madra-Dubh remarked. "And to think, some good news from them for once."

This news was anything but good for Raphael. His shoulders fell, and he had to duck his head to hide his face. He well remembered what Erian had said during the Convocation: if food came, Raphael would have to give the baby back. He sorrowed as he recalled agreeing to Erian's demand. But he hadn't known then! He couldn't have known what it would be like! He lifted his face and met Erian's eyes, but she did not look triumphant at all. She looked sad, and then she looked away.

Before anyone could say anything, there came a frantic shriek from the watchmouse at the bottom of the spiral staircase: "A black-robe! Coming up the stairs!"

Down inside the Cathedral, only yards away from the north spiral staircase to the High Reaches, Abbot Gregory noticed the tiny mouse sprinting in front of him but paid it no further mind. Something had been bothering him since he'd left the girl with the Infirmarer and the Infirmarer's donkey-sized dog Æthelred. It hadn't left him alone, this tantalizing sense that he almost knew what was going on, that he'd almost put it together, that if he'd just try a little harder, all of the strangeness at the Cathedral in the last few days would make sense. Unusual noises from the roofs after dark; small portions of food missing; cloths and parchment spirited away; a mysterious fuss in the cowshed; a starved, exhausted woman insisting she'd left her baby in the foundling box when no baby had been found by the brother on duty that night; and Brother John babbling about Baby Jesus in the rafters.

No, Brother John didn't say "baby Jesus up there," Abbot Gregory had realized. He'd just said "baby." *Baby up there.*

Gregory's mouth had suddenly gone dry and his heart had started pounding. He had come to himself with a start in the middle of the Kitchen Yard, with Nicholas of Bedford earnestly asking if he was all right. "Yes, yes," Gregory had babbled, "you'll excuse me for a moment, won't you?" and he took off for the Cathedral as fast as decorum would let him. What if John was right? was the question hammering inside his head. What if there really was a baby "up there?" It sounded ridiculous but what if someone had stolen the baby from the box at just the right moment and was hiding on the roofs, knowing that no one went up there in the winter?

So Gregory had pushed his way through the bedlam inside the Cathedral, half-convinced it was true, half-convinced he was going quite mad, and had nearly reached the stairs themselves when the watchmouse confirmed his trajectory and howled the warning. Up on Raphael's balcony everyone panicked. Raphael looked wildly from side to side, clutching the baby as he tried frantically to decide what to do. The monk's steps could be clearly heard, cracking sharply on the stone as he rapidly climbed. Raphael's fright soared with each report until he could no longer think properly. Without a word he grabbed the harness basket in his teeth, tucked the baby under a foreleg, and bolted for the second staircase at the other end of the balcony.

Erian and Madra-Dubh watched Raphael go in openmouthed amazement. To them it seemed the absolute end of the world as their eyes traveled from the staircase where Raphael disappeared to the empty niche where Raphael was supposed to stand. They had heard the monk reach the topmost step on the opposite staircase before Madra-Dubh's brain started working again.

"MADRA-DUBH CALLS DEFENSE!" he cried into the air. "THE GRAY-WINGS! TO ME!"

Abbot Gregory had barely taken a single step outside onto the balcony when he was set upon by what he first thought was a plague of demons. If you've ever been in the middle of a city square when something disturbs the pigeons pecking about on the ground, then you know it is a flapping, seething, roiling hurricane of flying feathers, sharp pointed beaks, and bright little eyes swirling dizzily around your head, making you want to do nothing more than throw your arms up over your face and run for cover. When the pigeons descended furiously upon him, Gregory did just that. He staggered back into the stairwell with a

shout of "God in Heaven!", waving his arms helplessly about, and nearly decided to forget this whole ridiculous mess. But something stopped him short as he was just a few steps down. It was the image of a tincture bottle; just a small, crude ceramic tincture bottle, balanced on the edge of the balcony.

Chapter Seventeen

Madra-Dubh and Erian had seen the tincture bottle too. Madra-Dubh lunged out with his arms but could not reach it, fixed as he was on the wall by his counterbalancing stone. Erian, who'd just started to follow Raphael in his wild flight down the stairs, skidded to a halt and reversed direction. She was only a few feet from the evidence when she saw Gregory cautiously making another foray onto the balcony. She yelped, "Gray-Wings! Again!" and once more those intellectually limited but undeniably gallant birds swooped down, beating their wings around Gregory's head as fiercely as they could.

Gregory wasn't going to be stopped this time. He threw his arms over his face and plunged forward even though he was half-blinded by the onslaught. But Erian was even more determined. By the time Gregory reached the lip of the balcony, the tincture bottle was gone, falling gracefully down the West Façade until it vanished soundlessly in a little pile of snow far below.

The pigeons suddenly peeled up and away into the air. Gregory clung to the railing, peering over the edge, but the pigeon attack had so discomfited him that he'd started to believe he'd imagined seeing the bottle. He turned around and took a long look at the balcony. Nothing moved. There was nothing unusual to note, except the behavior of the pigeons, and that might simply have been due to his sudden appearance. It was merely a windswept frozen balcony on the West Façade, that's all it was. And it was absolutely impossible that a baby could survive in such conditions.

Gregory marveled at his own foolishness. He paced slowly across the balcony to the stairwell on the other side, promising himself he'd get some more rest after the Christmas season was over.

Of course, you and I know that during the entire time Abbot Gregory stood on that balcony, he stood right next to an empty niche where a chimère ought to have been. But it is much more difficult to see something that *isn't* there than something that *is,* especially if, like the Abbot, you're so accustomed to seeing it that in fact you do even if you don't. This may sound very confusing but it happens all the time. Gregory hadn't noticed that Raphael was gone because to Gregory it was simply impossible that a chimère could move at all. And once you truly believe something to be "impossible," then your mind will refuse to see "the impossible" even if "the impossible" is happening directly in front of your nose.

Now, as it happened, "the impossible" was even then huddled at the base of the very stairwell that Gregory was entering. Raphael had managed to get the harness on by himself, carefully propping the baby up against the wall with his tail as he struggled with the straps and buckles. The baby, having a full belly, was dropping gently off to sleep and accepted this without protest. Mere steps beyond them, out in the light, dozens of people rushed back and forth carrying things and shouting instructions to each other at the top of their lungs. Raphael hoped fervently that he and the baby would not be noticed, tucked back in the dark stairwell. But if they were seen, then his only chance would be to somehow dash past all those people and hide somewhere outside the Cathedral until things calmed or it got dark or . . . *I'll think of something,* Raphael thought, trying to be brave even though he didn't feel brave at all. It was at that instant, of course, that he heard Abbot Gregory's steps on the top stair, coming down.

Now we must leave Raphael for a moment because across the Yard, in the Infirmary, something rather important was happening. The Dormitory watchmouse hiding there (yes, that same one from Raphael's visit to the Scriptorium), made reckless by his discovery of the baby's mother, had realized to his horror that he was now exposed in the middle of the floor. This ordinarily would not be a significant problem, as mice are very small and are frequently overlooked in the press of business. In fact, the Infirmarer himself had unknowingly stepped right over the watchmouse on his way out to the Kitchen to fetch a cup of broth for Juliana. All would have been well except that right in the middle of the doorway out, left behind to guard the sleeping patient, was the Infirmarer's dog Æthelred.

The watchmouse realized that he was in very bad trouble indeed. Æthelred was the size of a donkey, with the shaggy fur of a lion and, it appeared to the casual observer, more teeth than a shark. But, worst of all, Æthelred was mean. While mice and dogs are not friends, there is an understanding between them that if the mice do not interfere with people or people's things, the dogs will leave the mice alone. Shockingly, Æthelred chose not to adhere to this unspoken compact. He implacably viewed all mice as the enemy, an enemy to be searched out without mercy even in their homes. The list of his victims was mournfully long. And now he was blocking the watchmouse's only way out.

The watchmouse was sizing up the situation (which mostly meant estimating the distance between himself and Æthelred's teeth) just as Æthelred spotted him. The enormous beast levitated slowly up to his feet like he was being lifted by wires. Stiff-legged, staring fixedly, he hunched his shoulders at the mouse and growled.

The watchmouse felt his heart give one mighty wallop against his ribs. He knew without doubt that there was no place in the Infirmary to run. He allowed himself one moment to regret his impetuousness and to grieve for his family. But as the watchmouse motto is "Never say die," when he was finished, he gritted his teeth and rose to his hind legs, standing as tall as he could.

"Have a care, Æthelred," he shouted, "I've important news for the Cathedral. Let me pass."

Æthelred looked surprised—the only time mice ever spoke to him was to plead unsuccessfully for their lives—but then his eyes narrowed suspiciously behind the matted hair that mostly covered his bony face. "What's this! What's this!" he coughed. "Thief in the Infirmary asks me to stand aside?" The very thought infuriated the dog. His lips slowly peeled back from his teeth and he took a menacing step forward.

The watchmouse gulped but stood his ground. "It's about the missus," he called out, gesturing up at Juliana, who dozed fitfully in the bed behind him. "Her baby's up in the Cathedral—I've got to tell them. The black-robes would want it!" The watchmouse shook with terror as Æthelred stalked implacably toward him. In desperation, he shouted, "I cry Havoc, Æthelred!"

"What does the Havoc mean to me?" snarled Æthelred and lunged. The watchmouse leaped backward just in time. The snarling jaws snapped shut inches from his nose, the wind of Æthelred's roar blowing his fur back. The mouse saw his chance and fled for the door. Behind him Æthelred scrabbled for footing on the wooden floor, howling in rage as he skidded headlong into Juliana's bed. He knocked it a good two feet over before he regained his balance and leaped after the watchmouse, who was running faster than he had ever run before in his life. The mouse hurtled straight into the Yard, heedless of the horses and wagons and people milling about, darting this way and that to avoid hooves and wagon wheels, hearing only the nightmarish baying of Æthelred mere inches behind.

Pack and wagon horses are generally very stolid animals but the sight of a mouse skittering frantically way down around their feet is enough to startle even them, especially when it is immediately followed by a huge hairy beast bawling threats and curses. Straightaway, the Yard erupted into a pandemonium of rearing, shrieking horses bolting in all directions. Through the chaos of overturning carts, shouting humans, and toppling bags, the watchmouse and Æthelred continued their deadly race. The watchmouse dodged and ducked and twisted over carts and through flailing feet all the way across the Yard but Æthelred stayed with him, gaining ground until the watchmouse felt the dog's hot breath on his back. It would only be a moment until Æthelred caught him and that would be the end.

The mouse's strength was about to fail when he reached the front steps of the West Façade. He leaped up from stair to stair, gasping for breath, thinking that any moment he would feel the dog's jaws closing around him. But behind him Æthelred had stumbled, and that gave the mouse a few critical seconds to bolt through the Great Portal and look desperately for a place to hide. The first thing he saw was a well of shadow along the wall, a place to disappear—and he ran for it.

The shadow was the staircase where Raphael and the baby huddled. At that moment Raphael was fearfully gathering the sleeping baby up in his arms, preparing to flee, as Abbot Gregory descended step by step toward them. But just as Raphael tensed himself for the escape he saw the sudden tumult at the Great Portal. Through the uproar of people yelling and running about dropping packages Raphael instantly recognized the watchmouse racing toward him. He understood everything a moment later when he saw Æthelred lunge through the Great Portal in bawling pursuit.

In that instant, the chimère had to decide what to do. He could escape undetected with the baby while the Great Portal was in turmoil. Or he could stay to help the watchmouse, even though he'd certainly be discovered by the monk.

It really wasn't much of a choice at all. As the watch-mouse skidded into the stairwell and collapsed, his sides heaving, Raphael tucked the baby well behind him, flared his wings out, reared up to his full height and roared.

Instead of a helpless exhausted mouse in that stairwell Æthelred found a fearsome defender, a huge and terrifying creature half-dragon, half-lion, with vast wings that boomed like sails in a storm and claws that gleamed like knives in the gloom. As you know by now, Æthelred was a bully, and, like most bullies suddenly faced with superior force, Æthelred's attitude about the chase changed instantaneously. With a yelp he tried to reverse direction. He succeeded only in tan-gling himself up in his pie-plate feet and catapulting head over tail completely past Raphael to end up sprawled upside down across the bottom steps. Raphael dropped to all fours and whipped around after the dog, his head low and ears back, hissing savagely. He took a threatening step toward Æthelred. At the sound of Raphael's razor claws ticking on the stone Æthelred flailed his limbs frantically to right him-self and sprinted up the stairs, howling again but with pure cowardly fear this time.

Raphael watched Æthelred disappear up the steps and then looked down when he felt a tapping. It was the watch-mouse, still tumbled in a little heap between the chimère's feet. "Fancy that," gasped the mouse weakly. "Just the folks I'm wanting to see."

"No time," Raphael said. He checked the baby, still securely wrapped in his tail. Despite the fury of the past few moments the baby remained sound asleep. Just as a shout of "Hey! Hey! Ouch!" and a loud scrabbling, bonking sound came down from the stairwell overhead, Raphael tucked the baby and the mouse in his harness basket, said "Hold on!" over his shoulder and bounded straight up the stairs after Æthelred.

Chapter Eighteen

hat Raphael did may not make a lot of sense at first glance, but if you think about it for a moment, you'll agree that he was turning into a very clever chimère indeed. Raphael knew that the noise of his confrontation with Æthelred would draw the attention of every human in the Cathedral. In this he was absolutely right; from the Great Portal and the Nave both monks and visitors were advancing on the stairwell in a curious mob. To try to get through them would be impossible. But Raphael guessed that Æthelred would distract the monk coming down the stairs just enough to give him time to get past both of them up to the safety of the High Reaches. So he bundled both of his small passengers into his basket and took his chances.

He was absolutely right again. Æthelred, flying up the stairs, had met Abbot Gregory coming down in the fabled manner of the unstoppable force meeting the immovable object. There was a terrific collision (thus the shouts of "Hey!" and "Ouch!" that Raphael had heard), whereupon Æthelred had tried to climb straight up Abbot Gregory in much the same way that a person climbs a ladder. Considering that the dog weighed nearly as much as the Abbot, this only resulted in knocking them both flat on their backs. Gregory was forced to wrestle the screeching, thrashing beast off him to avoid being smothered alive. Occupied as he was, he did not notice the slender flare-winged form that vaulted silently over him into the shadows of the stairs above.

Safe up on the balcony, Raphael skidded to a halt before an astonished Erian and Madra-Dubh. He carefully reached up behind himself and gathered the watchmouse into one gentle paw. When the watchmouse felt the stone of the balcony under his feet, he bowed gravely to Raphael, saying, "Much obliged for the stand-up, guv'nor; thought I was a goner for a while," and then he turned to Erian and quite formally told her his news.

Erian's expression of shock and dismay turned to joy when she heard that the baby's mother had returned. She spun to Madra-Dubh, her face alight, and began to say something to the gargoyle, but Madra-Dubh shook his head and gestured toward Raphael. Erian looked back at the chimère, and her words turned to ashes in her mouth.

For Raphael was holding the baby in his arms and crying silently. He rocked back and forth with the child clasped to his chest, his face laid softly against the baby's, for quite a long time. And then he lifted his head to Erian and said only, "I know."

"Go over the rooftops to the Cloister," said Madra-Dubh gently. "No one will see you."

And that is what Raphael did. He put the baby in his harness basket, taking good care to tuck the blanket securely around its sleeping form, because the trip they were about to take would be a cold one; and then he vaulted up the stone wall behind the balcony, foot over foot, wings over tail, climbing higher and higher up the great gray tower of the West Façade, until he clung to the very topmost stone and the world lay spread around him like a wheel. Even though he knew the baby was sleeping, he stayed there for a few moments as if to show the baby the sight. Far below them tiny shapes bustled about the Square, people and horses, carts and wagons; flags for the night's celebration furled and snapped; dogs danced, and children tossed balls to each other. From the Yard, Nicholas of Bedford's caravan, now empty of its goods, began to move slowly into the streets. But to Raphael no sound came but the cold singing of the wind. He turned around, looking at the houses that clustered around the Cathedral as if for protection, each with its tiny garden and smudge of fire-smoke above. Beyond the houses he saw the Abbey's orchards and past them the fields, stretching gold and brown into the distance, and at the very edge of the world he could just see the sheep, coming to the folds in a solemn procession. All of these things seemed to Raphael to be turning around him, held firmly in place by the great building beneath his feet. It was a breathtaking vision. He would have gladly stayed there for hours, but he knew that the baby would soon awaken, and so he spread his wings like an eagle and leaped down to the Nave roof.

The crossing of the Nave took very little time. Raphael was only slowed by flat sheets of ice, tricky to negotiate even if you're standing on the ground rather than a hundred feet up on a sloping surface; but he moved with great care, knowing the preciousness of his cargo, and reached the south end of the Transept without incident. Below him were the Cloister buildings, tucked snugly under the arm of the Transept. In and out of them streamed a steady flow of monks, servants, and visitors, all deep in preparation for the Midnight Mass. Not one of them looked up to the roofs where a single chimère stood waiting. As soon as there was a small pause in the activity, Raphael bounded down to the roof of the Dormitory and raced for the small stone building at the end.

This was Abbot Gregory's little house. It was attached to the Dormitory but could be closed off from it, because the Abbot's duties often required solitude and quiet. Inside it were two rooms: the Abbot's sleeping quarters, bare except for a single bed, some wall hooks for clothing, and a place to kneel in prayer; and the Abbot's office. It was to the office that Raphael took the baby. In front of the warm fireplace there Raphael carefully removed his harness, placing the little basket down with great care. He retucked the blanket to make sure that the baby would stay warm. And he lay down next to the sleeping baby, his head on his paws, until he heard people coming up to the door.

There seemed to be two of them, one of whom was very excited about something. Raphael quietly slipped out the window he'd opened and huddled on the roof to watch them. They were both monks, he saw. One was limping.

"Please, Edgar, not now," the limping one said to the other. "I've got to fetch Master Nicholas's gold because the man is waiting, I have a thousand other things to do and no time to do them, and your dog just tried to kill me."

"But she is gone," spluttered the other indignantly.

"*Who* is gone, Edgar?" said the limping one, who we know was Abbot Gregory, in a long-suffering voice. He fished a massive black iron key from the ring hung from a cord around his waist and fiddled with the door. The door grudgingly  shuddered open and the Abbot stepped inside just as the other monk, whom we also know was the Infirmarer, said,

"The woman who claimed she'd lost the baby. Now they're both gone."

The Abbot stopped dead halfway into the room. "Oh, you're wrong," said Gregory without any surprise at all. "See? Here's the baby now."

Chapter Nineteen

Raphael, listening from his perch on the roof, felt as if he'd been struck a fearful blow. The baby's mother was gone! He'd given the baby back, but the mother had gone! Where could she be? What should he do now?

Where, in fact, had Juliana gone? To answer that question we must go back in time a little bit, back to when the watchmouse and Æthelred had their confrontation on the floor of the Infirmary. When Æthelred charged, he misjudged the distance between himself and the mouse; as his jaws snapped on empty air, he was carried by the force of his attack straight into the bed where Juliana restlessly slept. Æthelred paid this no mind, because he was awash in rage and could think of nothing but destroying the mouse who dared defy him. But the violent shock of the enormous hound striking the bed woke the young woman in the midst of a terrible dream. She sat up, her heart pounding with fear, and remembered that she must search for her child.

Now, losing a child is just about the very worst thing that can happen to anyone (go ahead and ask your mother about the time she lost you in the grocery store), and Juliana was ill with exhaustion and hunger. When she left the bed and walked unsteadily from the Infirmary into the Yard, she was a pitiable sight. Her hair had come undone and lay wildly about her shoulders, her shawl dragged behind her upon the ground, her face was aglow with fever. So when she placed one trembling hand on the shoulder of a monk who had not seen Juliana's earlier collapse, the monk was completely taken aback.

"Good woman!" exclaimed Brother Michael. "Take your hand away!"

"Please," said Juliana, "I've lost my baby here. Please help me find him." She clung to the monk's robe even as he tried to twitch it disdainfully back from her. "I left him here but now he's gone."

"Have you lost your senses?" snapped Brother Michael. Now, he knew better than to be so unkind, but he'd mistakenly decided that preparations for a Christmas celebration were much more important than helping someone in distress. (You'll find that even nowadays people make this very same mistake.) He continued tugging at his robe even as Juliana held on to it, and the sight of this unseemly tug-of-war drew the attention of several townspeople in the Yard. In moments a little group had gathered around the two.

"Please help me," Juliana kept repeating. She looked imploringly around the circle of staring bystanders. "I've lost my baby here, someone has taken him."

"She's mad," whispered one fat-faced goodwife to another. "I've seen things like this before."

"Look at her clothing, her hair!" hissed a third person in tones of righteous outrage. "Does the woman have no propriety?"

"And in an Abbey, no less!" "And on Christmas Eve, what's more!" "She's mad, I tell you." "Mad, mad." And all around Juliana the whispers grew and multiplied. Finally someone said, "We had better get the Watch—she might hurt someone."

At the mention of the Watch—the town's police—Juliana's face grew white. Her hand dropped away from the monk's robe and she took a few hesitant steps back. "Please," she said quietly, "I won't hurt anyone. You see, I've—"

"Hold her," murmured a townsman. "I'll fetch the Watch."

Now Brother Michael finally regretted his ill temper and said, "Wait a moment," but by then it was too late, as Juliana had turned and fled. She ran as best she could away from the threatening faces and grasping hands out of the Yard and into the town streets, where people pointed and stared at her heedless flight. Juliana knew that to fall in the hands of the Watch was a terrible thing. She could end up in gaol if they thought her mad. Her only thought was to escape, to find someplace safe, someplace where people would help her find her baby, for she knew it was true that she had left him at the Abbey and something terrible had happened there. Who would help her? Where could she go? In her anguish she thought of the one place where we all wish to go when we are sick or hurt and need help.

She would go home.

So Juliana ran, ran till she reached the edge of the town, with her fevered mind focused only on going home, where her parents would take her in and help her. If she were not so ill she would have known that she could not walk there herself. The village where her mother and father lived was many miles away. But when people are sick and frightened, they often do not think in the way that is best. Juliana set out alone on that rutted path of frozen mud that led away from the town, toward her childhood home, without food, or water, or even a proper coat, all in the hope of finding help for herself and her lost child.

She did not get far.

No more than an hour later, Nicholas of Bedford and two of his guards were traveling along that same road, trying to catch up with the emptied pack and wagon train that had left well ahead of them. With them traveled a chest of gold strapped to Nicholas's horse. This was the Abbey's payment for the caravan goods (which gold, you will recall, originated as Earl Odo's misguided attempt to pay off God for what he considered to be an unspeakable sin). One of the guards had just issued a stream of particularly spirited invective about the condition of the road when Nicholas's horse saw something in the ditch, thought briefly about it, and shot about six feet to the left without so much as a by-your-leave.

Needless to say, Nicholas did not go with the horse. He hit the ground and bounced into the ditch. By the time the guards had managed to pull around their own spooked horses and fetch Nicholas's, the merchant had found exactly what his horse had noticed so dramatically.

"It's a girl," he said, rubbing his bottom as he looked up at the guards. "And she's alive." (This was by no means a fore-gone conclusion in the Middle Ages.) "And she's holding a letter."

"What's it say?" asked one guard, who was a little smarter than the other.

Nicholas studied the crabbed lettering closely. As he read, he remembered receiving this very same letter from the priest in the tiny village about another day up the road. Old parents, wanting their daughter to come home. He looked carefully at the girl slumped insensible in the ditch, as if she'd dropped in midstep. It didn't seem to be the plague.

She just looked starved and exhausted; a condition he'd seen before in his travels, and, despite his best hopes, knew he'd see again.

"How convenient," he said mildly. "She is headed right in our direction."

Chapter Twenty

So we leave Juliana in Nicholas's care, bundled upon the back of his horse as they caught up with the wagon train, and then settled by Nicholas himself into a warm bed of hay and blankets in the back of an open cart.

At the Cathedral, however, things were not going nearly so well. Raphael had been struck into a panic by the news he'd overheard at the Abbot's house. His first impulse was to take the baby back—the mother was gone, wasn't she? But the events of the past three days made the young chimère think twice about his actions. He could not steal the baby undetected—hadn't a monk just been on his very balcony? And, more importantly, the monks now had food. They would care for the baby just as they had cared for the little boys that had played around him for years in the High Reaches. And finally he admitted to himself that he'd agreed, during the Convocation, to give the baby up if the monks could care for it. He simply could not go back on his word now.

There did not seem to be anything he could do. That was what Raphael told himself at first, leaving the roof of the Abbot's house and clambering over the Dormitory to the Transept and finally onto the Nave. But something inside him disagreed. The small voice of his conscience, the same voice he'd crushed when Madra-Dubh and Erian had argued with him after the fiasco in the cowshed, now spoke with an unmistakable clarity. If you'd given the baby back then, the voice said, the baby would have its mother now. If you hadn't tried to keep the baby when you knew you shouldn't, then all would be well. This is your fault and you must try to repair it.

I must find the baby's mother, Raphael suddenly understood. His claws dug deeply into the ice and he began to run, tearing across the slick sloped roofs without thought. It is my responsibility and no one else's.

But he also knew that he could not do this alone. He must seek the counsel of Madra-Dubh and Erian this time, for they could help him with what seemed to be impossible problems. Where to begin the search? Who would search, as the sun had not yet set? And—most importantly—if the baby's mother were found, how would she be told where the baby was?

When he arrived back on his balcony, Raphael was in

quite a state. Madra-Dubh had to shout at him to calm down and be quiet because he was making absolutely no sense at all. "What are ye babbling about, she's *gone?*" shrieked the gargoyle. "If this is some sort of joke, newtnose—"

"It's not a joke and it's not a trick," Raphael pleaded. "I heard the monk say it to the other. 'The woman who claimed she lost the baby. Now they're both gone.' That's what he said, Madra-Dubh, I swear! We have to find her!"

"She could be anywhere," said Erian grimly. She'd been looking forward to going home and seeing her great-great-great-great-great-grandchildren, after days up on the frozen windswept balcony, and her mood was not a good one. It did not, however, affect her ability to think. "She was last at the Infirmary. If she left through the Yard, then some of our people might have seen her. We'll send out some pigeons, ask the mice down there. Where's that Dormitory watch-mouse, the one who saw her in the Infirmary? We need to find out what she looks like. Although, the Architect knows, it's hard enough to tell them apart." From her side a young sentry mouse sprinted for the stairwell.

Madra-Dubh spluttered at this. "What blasted good is that going to do?" he growled. "Suppose we do find the mother. What are we going to do then?"

"I will think of that in a moment," replied Erian with forbidding determination. "It all depends on where she is."

The Dormitory watchmouse had recovered from his narrow escape and quickly described Juliana for the pigeons. From the balcony, a great cloud of them scattered through the air in all directions, some arrowing to the streets of the town, some spiraling down to the Yard. On the ground, the mice spread out in waves to search every corner of the Cathedral. It did not take long before pigeons began to return to the balcony, breathlessly bearing the news that Juliana had left the Yard—run down the High Street—was last seen at the edge of the town, on the road that wound through the fields to the horizon. Madra-Dubh shook his head at this but Erian shot him a warning look. "We'll wait for the forward scouts," she said. "Maybe she will return."

But at last a tired and much-bedraggled pigeon landed before Erian and gasped out his tidings. He had seen a female human with long red hair, dressed in black clothing, in the back of a cart about two miles hence, going away.

Madra-Dubh said firmly, "That's the end of it, then. She's gone."

Guilt and shame rushed over Raphael in a wave. He knew now what it was like to give up a baby, and he could not bear it that someone should have to undergo such a thing due to his own selfishness. "No! There must be something we could do!" he protested. He ran to his niche and sprang to the top of the railing, flaring his wings like he could leap from there directly to Juliana. "The pigeons can get there. What if the pigeons tried to tell her? Or the mice, maybe some of the mice along the road—"

Erian shook her head sadly. "We can't talk to the humans directly, Raphael. Nor can the pigeons. We can understand them, but we've tried and tried and they can't or won't understand us. We think that the only ones who can speak to them are the ones they made themselves—like you or Madra-Dubh."

"Then I'll do it!" Raphael said. "I'll speak to the monks. Or I'll go find her myself!"

"You're bleeding daft!" shouted Madra-Dubh, who'd reached the end of his tattered patience. "I suppose we're not in enough trouble already—now you want to start running around town like the tinker's loose goat! First of all, the monks will destroy you if you try to speak to them—ask the Yard mice, there's already talk in the town of a demon living in the Cathedral from the last time you did a parade round! And the caravan's already miles away, Raphael. Not even your lizard legs could carry you that far fast enough. The only way you'd be able to get to the blasted woman would be if you were like a pigeon, if you could—if you could—"

There was an achingly long pause as both Erian and Madra-Dubh thought of the exact same thing at the exact same time. Unable to stop themselves, they turned and looked at Raphael in unison.

Raphael said, "What?"

"Oh no," Madra-Dubh said. "Oh no, Erian, it's a fairy story."

"What?" demanded Raphael.

"It's in the Archives," said Erian gravely.

"It's a bleeding *footnote* in the bleeding Archives!" bellowed Madra-Dubh.

"WHAT?" shouted Raphael at the top of his lungs.

"We think chimères can sometimes fly," said Erian.

Chapter Twenty-one

hy, of course I can," said Raphael with an expression of dawning delight. "I've got wings, don't I?"

"And I've got legs but you don't see me dancing a jig in the middle of the Square," snapped Madra-Dubh. "Just because you've got something doesn't mean you're meant to use it. Erian, what happened with Parsifal was a long time ago, even if it did happen at all." Madra-Dubh winced as soon as those last words left his mouth. He cursed himself for being foolish, because he knew what Raphael would do once he said it. And, surely enough, Raphael leaped upon the mention of Parsifal.

"Tell me about Parsifal," he begged Erian. "The Alchemist said he was a chimère like me. He said that Parsifal had a Noble Task. Please, you've got to tell me."

Erian thought hard for a long moment. It was true that

the story was only, as Madra-Dubh
put it, a "footnote in the
Archives." But she also believed in her heart that the
story of Parsifal was true.
And, finally, she could not
fairly refuse to tell it to
Raphael, as the story about Parsifal
and his Noble Task was one of the reasons why she had allowed Raphael to
keep the baby at all.

"Parsifal was a Guardian at the very
beginning of the Cathedral, when the foun-
dation stones were being laid along the Transept and the
Crossing, and the great stones for the piers were dragged
across the country," she began. "He was the very first
chimère carved, a magnificent eagle, and he was put in a
place of honor. All the other chimères who came after him
regarded Parsifal with great respect, for he was wise beyond
his years. In time he became the Great Guardian and took his
place among the other Great Elders of the Cathedral.

"It happened, as the Aisle walls were climbing to the sky,
that the humans began one of their wars. A woman and her
children came one night to the Cathedral and begged sanctu-
ary. They were great ones—you could see from the nobility

of their bearing—and they were in danger from an enemy army. The Abbot took them in, despite the great risk, and the Cathedral hoped that the war would pass us by.

But that was not to be and the Cathedral came under siege from the enemy army. The local lords came to defend us, and there was much fighting, a terrible thing of fear, and sword, and fire by day and by night. The Guardians followed Parsifal in doing what they could. They loosened stones to cast down upon the enemy and deflected their arrows . . . but in the end it seemed all was lost. One night Parsifal saw one of the enemy come to the Cathedral under the white flag of parley. He listened as the enemy warned the Abbot to surrender, because the soldiers that had been sent to rescue the woman and her children had been deceived. Misled by the enemy's spies, the rescuers had gone to the wrong village.

Parsifal knew where that place was, as his carver had come from that village. He saw that their only hope was to find the rescuers and lead them back to the Cathedral. He said to the others that it was his Noble Task to try to reach them, even if he failed. So he climbed to the very top of the Cathedral, spread out his wings, and cast himself into the air, even though he knew that he would almost certainly fall."

In a very small voice, Raphael asked, "Did he?"

"No!" said Erian triumphantly. "The Archives say that the gargoyles and chimères saw a great eagle shape soar into the sky until it vanished into the darkness. And not a day later, the soldiers came to rescue the woman and her children, the siege was lifted and the Cathedral saved. So the story began that if a Noble Task arises, all of us are given the strengths to fulfill it. Then, and only then, is a chimère able to fly."

"But where is Parsifal now?" Raphael said. "Why isn't he here to help us?"

Erian shook her head. "He never returned," she said. "No one knows what happened to him. And that is why there is no Great Guardian for the Cathedral, as there is a Great Sentinel among the gargoyles and a Great Elder for the mice and the pigeons. No one could replace a Guardian of such courage. It was agreed among the Elders left behind that this story would not be told unless there was a Noble Task at stake. Parsifal's story could mislead others into doubting the First Rule. They might ignore their proper place in the Cathedral and foolishly attempt things that they could not do."

"Fly, for instance," growled Madra-Dubh pointedly to Raphael. "You can't do it, newtnose. This isn't a siege and you're not Parsifal."

"But I do have a Noble Task," Raphael rejoined. "I know I do. Erian said I had one, too, during the Convocation. And you never disagreed!" He paused and took a deep breath. "Madra-Dubh, Erian, you are the Elders and this time I will listen to you. If you tell me to stay on the

High Reaches, I will. But please give me the chance to set things right."

Alarmed by Raphael's determination, Madra-Dubh saw no other course than to speak as brutally as possible to the young chimère. He did it because he was afraid for Raphael, and fear makes people finally say out loud the things that are ordinarily too awful to contemplate. And what Madra-Dubh was contemplating was very awful indeed. If you recall, earlier on in this story I mentioned that gargoyles—and like them, chimères—were afraid of two things, but I only named one. Freezing water, which expands in hairline cracks in stone until it shatters the thing that hosts it, is the first fear. The second is, of course, falling. Stone may be very hard but it is also brittle and, when dropped from a high enough place, it will explode into a thousand thousand pieces, so many that they can never be reassembled. This was the risk that Raphael took. If the story of Parsifal was not true—or even if it was, if Raphael did not, in fact, have a Noble Task—then he could not fly, and Raphael would meet that dreadful end.

The thought frightened Madra-Dubh more than anything else he had ever faced. "You could fall," Madra-Dubh said fiercely. "You could die." Erian nodded miserably in agreement. "If we were wrong about your Noble Task," she said, "if I was wrong, you will fall." Then they both fell silent. It was, in the end, no one's choice but Raphael's.

"I know," Raphael told them simply. "But you understand, I have to try."

So he did.

They chose the North Tower as his launching place. The winds were rising, and Madra-Dubh argued that Raphael should not go that night, but wait until the next; he feared that the oncoming storm could dash Raphael to the ground even if, by a miracle, the chimère's wings did bear him up. But Raphael would not be dissuaded. With every moment, the wagon carrying the baby's mother drew farther away. There was no other chance, he said, but to go just as soon as darkness fell.

The three spoke little as the grim afternoon passed into a stormy twilight and the moon rose with aching slowness over the Cathedral. As soon as the silver disk had cleared the Spire, Raphael left his friends behind on his wind-scoured balcony and climbed foot over foot, wings over tail, up the soaring stone of the North Tower. He did not hesitate even though the ice was slick and treacherous underfoot and the freezing wind intensified its fury. Clouds driven by the mounting gale boiled over the moon until he found himself ascending in almost complete darkness. As he climbed, Raphael could hear nothing except the roaring gusts and could see almost nothing except the faint shape of the Tower summit looming above him. Yet he continued on, foot by slow foot, digging his claws into the ice as he scaled the vertical stone, refusing to give up even as the storm shrieked and tore at his wings and howled its mockery in his ears.

You're going to fall, the wind screamed. *You're going to fall. And when you do, you'll shatter like glass on the cobblestones because you know that chimères can't really fly—*

"NO!" Raphael shouted. Ferocious whips of sleet ripped his cry away into the bleak night. Raphael gritted his teeth, clinging to the rough stone until he gathered enough strength to move another leg out, grasp a foothold, haul himself up another length. He fought for each agonizing inch but it seemed as if the Cathedral itself resisted him. After the third time he slid helplessly down the Tower face, each time ending up farther back than the last, Raphael began to lose hope.

It was then that he truly understood what he had done when he'd claimed the baby as his Noble Task. He realized at last that Noble Tasks are made up not of sentiment but of struggle, a test of everything in his heart and will, and that the time had passed to refuse the trial. He gathered himself again and lunged upward. Once, twice, three times, his claws biting deeply, ignoring the wind-whipped granules of ice and snow that blasted him from seemingly all directions at once, he bounded up the sheer precipice until there finally was no further to go. He had reached the top.

Raphael clung to the topmost stone for a moment, trembling from his effort, and waited, as Erian had told him, for the wind to diminish. In a brief shaft of moonlight, he saw

below him the empty expanse of the Square, the houses huddled against its edge, and then, far ahead, the thin glowing
ribbon of the road he must find and follow. He took a deep
breath as the wind fell away. And then he spread his wings
and leaped out into the air.

He fell for a horrifying minute. The black ground rushed
up at his face. In terror Raphael brought down his wings in a
mighty percussive stroke. The air whistled beneath them and
suddenly Raphael was flung upward into the sky, his wings
booming, scything through the storm higher and higher with
each beat. In shock and amazement and, finally, sheer laughing joy, Raphael circled the very heights of the Tower,
smoothly cutting through the whipping cloud. He swooped
down and skimmed over his balcony—Madra-Dubh and Erian cheering madly as he passed—and then soared up above
the Square to orient himself to the road. He was so focused
upon finding that slender track that he did not pay enough attention to the storm. For Raphael had sprung out during a
brief lull in its fierceness, and lulls do not last forever.

Far behind his rising figure, in the fields, the dead stalks
shivered and then suddenly lay flat. A moment later the
limbs of the orchard trees bent forward violently. A keening
began at the pointed arc of the Lady Chapel to the east and
spread forward along the flanks of the Cathedral like a rush-
ing sea. It was the wind, returning as an avenging demon,
and it screamed against the stone until it crashed together

before the West Façade in a furious maelstrom. It struck Raphael with terrific force halfway over the Square and flipped him over as casually as you or I might flip a card.

Raphael struggled against the blow, trying to spread out his wings, and succeeded for a moment in righting himself. But before he could take another wingstroke, a second buffet of wind tossed him sideways and then he was really falling, tumbling end over end as he plunged downward, slammed forward and back so that he could no longer recognize which way was earth and which was sky. It would be mere seconds till he struck the cobblestones. In this time Raphael had but one thought. It was a sorrow, but not for himself; for the baby's mother and her child, who would now never see each other again because he had failed.

And there we will leave Raphael, falling from the sky . . .

Chapter Twenty-two

For inside the Cathedral a most strange and thrilling sound was growing.

◆ ◆ ◆   It was a small sound at first; a slight, singing tone, barely loud enough to hear, as if someone in another room were drawing a finger around the top of a wineglass. And then it grew. It grew until it was an insistent harmony, something so lovely it would break your heart with the hearing of it; but underneath there was also a shivering, as if an entire room of wineglasses were trembling as one. In the Cathedral, the single monk still working stopped what he was doing.

Brother Michael wasn't supposed to be there; Abbot Gregory had told all the monks to search the town in hope of finding Juliana before the Midnight Mass. But Michael could not resist giving the statues one last polish and so had slipped back inside the Cathedral when no one was looking.

He was alone in the Lady Chapel when the ringing, shaking sound all around him became so loud that he had to put his hands over his ears. He looked up at the three stained-glass angels above the little

statue of the mother and child and dropped his dusting rag. For all three were vibrating, shaking in their stone frames like cymbals struck with a sword.

The sound stopped.

Brother Michael, not knowing what else to do, picked up the dusting rag.

And then the center window flexed and sprang forward toward him with an explosion of shattering glass, and with it there came an astonishing, an amazing thundering of wings, and a blast of sound so clear and pure it rang like the trumpet that will someday sound the end of the world. Brother Michael cried out, covered his head with his dusting rag, and threw himself to the ground. He cowered in awestruck terror as a rush of wind roared past him and down the Choir and through the Transept and the Nave and the massive doors of the Great Portal blasted open in a heartbeat before it and then it was gone.

Chapter Twenty-three

Raphael was caught so gently, he didn't realize at first that he was still alive.

Actually the first thing he thought was: *That didn't hurt nearly as much as I thought it would,* and the second thing he thought was, *That really didn't hurt at all;* and then he stretched all his legs and wings out, with his eyes still tightly shut, and thought the third thing, which was, *You know, I don't think I'm dead.*

So he opened his eyes and saw what he was doing. Which was, in fact, sailing over the roofs of the town at a speed beyond belief, even given his earlier flight over the Cathedral. The view set him back a bit and he flailed every limb he had in a frantic scrabble to save himself. It was at that time a Voice remarked quite clearly inside his head (although no place else): "Don't be afraid."

Of course, hearing Voices inside your head is not something that helps one relax under any circumstances, so

Raphael redoubled his futile efforts to find something to run on and something to fly off of. The Voice repeated, patiently, "Don't be afraid. I have you."

"Who are you?" Raphael managed, hearing even as he spoke the wind of his flight tearing away the words. But the Voice, whatever it was, was unperturbed. "I was asked to help you. There is a Task to finish," it said.

"You know about that?" stuttered Raphael and was struck dumb by what happened next; for once soaring high above the rooftops, he suddenly screamed down toward the ground, the silver ribbon of roadway now thrust out before him, glowing faintly as ice in moonlight. Inches from the frozen mud he was caught up again and pushed forward, even faster this time, the wind tearing at his face like angry fingers. Crabbed skeletons of trees whipped by to either side. Raphael covered his eyes and whimpered.

"We must move very quickly now," the Voice said, somewhat apologetically. "It always seems to happen like that."

Raphael gulped as he was jerked to the left, avoiding a raven flapping slowly down the middle of the road. The huge black bird croaked a brief protest as he was left whipsawing in their wake. Raphael looked back and then forward again, because he'd caught a glimpse of a warm glow rising in a smudged red arc over the hill before him. The glow resolved into three separate burning circles as he sped toward it. Three fires, and around them a gathering of wagons, carts, and animals. The wind roar in his ears fell away as he circled above the protective huddle of Nicholas of Bedford's wagon train and began to descend.

"Are you ready?" asked the Voice.

"She is here," said Raphael. The words started out as a question but changed into something else as he spoke them.

The Voice remained silent. Raphael said, desperately, "You know what happened. Who are you? How do I tell her? She'll be afraid of me, she'll run away—"

"This is all part of the Noble Task," replied the Voice gently. Raphael was spiraled inexorably toward the bitter ground. Watching it rise, Raphael felt something break inside him.

"I don't know what a Noble Task is," he blurted out. "I thought I was doing the right thing before to take care of the baby but it turned out not to be the right thing at all, and everything has been so awful and frightening since then for everyone that I think whatever I do won't fix it, and it's all so terrible that it couldn't have been a Noble Task at all, not really."

"It's a hard thing to understand," said the Voice as it set Raphael gently down upon the turf. "Start at the beginning. Why did you take the baby, Raphael?"

"I thought it was my Noble Task," Raphael began, and then his shame crept out of its hiding place inside him, because he knew that there was another reason too. "It wasn't just about the famine. I took the baby because I thought it would protect me against the Silver Knight," he said miserably. "I thought that if the Knight saw me taking care of the baby, then he'd know I wasn't evil, and he wouldn't kill me. And I didn't tell Erian and the Convocation about the Knight, either, even though I knew I should have."

Raphael shrank into himself as he thought about his cravenness. The cold all around him was so fierce it burned.

The Voice asked quietly, "Then could your Noble Task truly lie somewhere else?"

Raphael tried to think of something noble he had done, but his actions seemed to have caused only pain and grief, to others and to himself. Yet maybe there was one thing, just one thing that he'd decided . . . "Was it—was it giving the baby back? Even though it hurt more than anything, even though I didn't want to do it, because it was the best for the baby, and for everyone else?"

"Now you are beginning to understand," said the Voice. "I think it is time for you to go."

Raphael looked over the wagons arrayed in tight circles around the guttering fires. A single wagon glowed a little more in the moonlight than the others. He knew that the baby's mother was there, and that he must go and speak to her. But something stopped him, a tremulous fear, one that was not merely for himself.

"She'll be afraid," he pleaded. "She'll run away. You could

make me fly. Make me something else, something beautiful, so I won't frighten her."

There was a little quiet. In time the Voice said, thoughtfully, "That I can do. But you may find that the woman has a special gift; she is able to see not only how things look, but how they really are."

"Please," repeated Raphael. And then again, simply, "Please."

"It is done," said the Voice. Raphael did not feel anything different, but walked forward nonetheless toward the slightly glowing wagon at the far side of the camp. Because if anything was to be taken as true, it was that Voice. And when he arrived, he carefully opened the wagon door clasp without fear, even though he himself saw only his claw working the mechanism.

Inside the wagon a sleepless Juliana gasped to see the cold frame of night appear before her eyes, and inside it, suddenly, a glow of white fire, coalescing into the form of a beautiful young man. The young man did nothing for a moment but look upon her. And then he said, quite earnestly, "Don't be afraid."

Chapter Twenty-four

I'm not afraid," breathed Juliana. "You are an angel."

Raphael hesitated, but then shook his head. "No," he admitted. "I'm not an angel. But I live in the Cathedral and I've come because of your baby."

Juliana's heart leaped with a wild hope. She rose to her knees. "Oh, please, is he all right? Where is he? Please tell me."

Raphael grieved in his heart to watch her, because he knew he was the one who had caused her so much pain. He almost could not speak for the shame of it. "I took him," he confessed. "When you left him at the Cathedral, I took him with me up into the High Reaches and I took care of him. But I kept him even after I knew I shouldn't, and that's why you couldn't find him, but I gave him back to the monks and now I've come to find you."

"He's all right," Juliana said, "the monks have him," and then she started to cry. They were tears of joy and relief, not hurt. Raphael wept too, but for another reason. After a moment Juliana lifted her face from her hands and studied Raphael.

"The High Reaches," she said quietly. "You do not look like this, I think. Not in truth."

She is able to see not only how things look, but how they really are, the Voice had said. Raphael felt a jolt of terror. *I mustn't let her know what I am,* he thought desperately. *Because if I do, she will believe that I am evil.* He struggled fiercely within himself. Visions of Juliana horrified, fleeing in terror upon a glimpse of his true appearance, all flashed by him in a single second. But Raphael had started to tell the truth and he simply couldn't bring himself to begin to lie now. He owed Juliana more than that for what he had done.

"Please don't make me," he said miserably. "I'm so ugly."

"Let me see you," asked Juliana.

And Raphael surrendered in his heart to her request. His shining countenance began to change as the light faded gently away from his form, revealing in time the long, snakelike neck, the dragon face, the sharp teeth and scythelike claws, the wings folded flat against his slender body, his long and lashing tail. Raphael in his true appearance huddled before the young woman. He waited for the inevitable shock and horror to cross her face.

But Juliana watched his transformation in silence. When it was finished, she came to him, raising her hand. Raphael flinched, but she ever so carefully reached out to touch his neck. "You are not ugly," she said, stroking him gently. "How can anyone who loves a child be ugly?"

Raphael looked up into her eyes and a light seemed to envelop him, a light so bright it filled the wagon and splashed out onto the frozen heath like the burning of a brilliant sun. They sat together, gazing at each other, for what seemed to Raphael an eternity of joy. It was broken all too soon by a startled shout from outside.

"You had best go," said Juliana. "As must I."

Raphael turned and stepped from the wagon. A thought struck him and he looked back at Juliana. "You won't tell anyone?" he pleaded.

A broad smile spread across her tearstained face. "Tell anyone?" she laughed. "They *already* think I'm mad."

Raphael fled into the darkness as the shouts came nearer. He had reached the edge of the camp when he felt a sharp warm wind swirl around him and suddenly he was in the air again, soaring over the wagons and fires below. The Voice said quietly, "Well done."

"Is it finished?" asked Raphael as the trees blurred past him. "Have I finished the Noble Task?"

"It is never really finished for any of us," replied the Voice, "for we are always asked to do it, over and over, loving others as we love ourselves, and sometimes more." At that moment they crested the little rise that led into the town, and the Cathedral appeared. It no longer loomed dark and cold. Instead, light blazed forth from every window, spreading across the Square from the open doors of the Great Portal as if to illuminate the world. The Cathedral's great bells pealed triumphantly through the wind. As Raphael drew closer, he caught a glimpse of a riot of color inside, paint and flags, gleaming gold and silver, the stained glass burning deep and bright, and, above it all, there was the glorious music that he remembered. But now it rose unrestrained through the spaces of the Cathedral and spilled boldly out into the sky. For Raphael had arrived at the start of the Midnight Mass, the night when the Cathedral sings out the new song of its jubilation, and Raphael felt overcome by its power as he was set gently down into his niche. By the time he realized what was happening, the warm wind had pulled away from him and was fast disappearing.

"Oh, please, don't leave," Raphael shouted into the air. "I have so much to ask you—"

"I will always be with you," came the fading response. "I am a guardian too, after all."

From across the balcony Erian rushed toward Raphael with great joy. Raphael swept her up into his embrace. At this point Madra-Dubh decided to speak up. Remember that a despondent Madra-Dubh had just seen Raphael return unharmed when his last vision was of his friend tumbling, uncontrolled, from the sky. He'd just had a great weight lifted miraculously from him. He was dazed with relief at seeing his friend again. And in this powerful moment, with all the things in the world that could possibly be said, Madra-Dubh could not help but be true to his kind. He bellowed out a perfectly gargoyle remark: "Who on earth were you babbling to, newtnose?"

But Raphael didn't hear him at first. Because Raphael, holding Erian up to the stars in one careful paw, was singing.

A f t e r w o r d

So that is where we leave them, Raphael and Madra-Dubh and Erian reunited on the balcony, with the Cathedral beneath them shining in the darkness. Not too long after Raphael's flight, a Convocation was called to name Raphael as Great Guardian of the Cathedral; but that is a story for another time.

What of the others, you ask? Juliana found her baby only hours later, as she convinced Nicholas of Bedford to ride her back to the Cathedral on his fastest horse. After her joyous reunion with her son (during which many people apologized profusely to Juliana for their unkind behavior), they both returned to Nicholas's wagon and pack train. Now while you might think, given the nature of this story, that Nicholas and Juliana fell in love on the trip to Juliana's village, in fact they didn't. But Nicholas would drop in on Juliana whenever his merchant travels took him by her little cottage, and they would spend an enjoyable time catching up with each other's news.

Juliana's baby was none the worse for his amazing adventure at the top of the Cathedral. In time he would grow up to become a monk and join an Abbey (although not Abbot Gregory's), where he would become a renowned illustrator of illuminated manuscripts. If you're ever in an antiquities shop or perhaps a museum which has medieval books, you might ask to examine one or two of their collection. Look very closely at the borders. You will know if you have found one of the books drawn by Juliana's son, because among the flowing leaves and strewn flowers there is always a tiny, kind-faced dragon hidden somewhere.

Abbot Gregory was enormously relieved when Juliana returned to claim the baby. But, as she didn't say a word about Raphael, the mystery of the baby's disappearance and then reappearance remained. Gregory promised himself he'd get down to the bottom of things as soon as he could. But in the Abbey's day-to-day press of business, at last even the conscientious Gregory forgot about the strange events. Except for one thing, that is: every now and then he'd wander up to the North Balcony on the West Façade and have a good long look around, hands on his hips and a puzzled expression on his face. The other monks regarded this as simply one of the Abbot's harmless eccentricities and continued, somewhat to Gregory's dismay, to reelect him Abbot.

In the life of the Cathedral itself, all was quickly restored to normal. The mouse societies and the pigeon tribes went back to their usual ways, living largely separate lives inside and out of the magnificent building. Yet a few things had changed, and these I will note before the story ends.

Brother Michael was never quite the same after his remarkable experience in the Lady Chapel the night of Christmas Eve. For despite his insistence that the stained-glass angel above the little statue had shattered, the window was found to be whole upon inspection, leaving Brother Michael convinced that he had seen a miracle (or heard it, at any rate). He began to spend less time polishing and more time praying and was considerably kinder to Brother John and everyone else as a result.

But unlike the glass angel, other denizens of the Cathedral had been forever altered. For example, where once there might have been faces of angry contempt carved into the stone columns and aisle walls, there were now only gentle expressions of sympathy and compassion. Moreover, even if a person were to search every inch of the Cathedral, a certain marble lizard was simply no longer to be found.

And finally, what of Æthelred, the Infirmarer's fearsome hound, the persecutor of the small and defenseless? His was the greatest transformation of all; for he never—not even *once*—bothered a mouse for the rest of his life, which was very long indeed.

THE END